Westfield Memorial Library
Westfield, New Jersey

PRAISE FOR WORLD GONE WATER

"Jaime Clarke's *World Gone Water* is so fresh and daring, a necessary book, a barbaric yawp that revels in its taboo: the sexual and emotional desires of today's hetero young man. Clarke is a sure and sensitive writer, his lines are clean and carry us right to the tender heart of his lovelorn hero, Charlie Martens. This is the book Hemingway and Kerouac would want to read. It's the sort of honesty in this climate that many of us aren't brave enough to write."

—TONY D'SOUZA, author of *The Konkans*

"This unsettling novel ponders human morality and sexuality, and the murky interplay between the two. Charlie Martens is a compelling antihero with a voice that can turn on a dime, from shrugging naiveté to chilling frankness. *World Gone Water* is a candid, often startling portrait of an unconventional life."

— J. ROBERT LENNON, author of *Familiar*

"Funny and surprising, *World Gone Water* is terrific fun to read and, as a spectacle of bad behavior, pretty terrifying to contemplate."

—ADRIENNE MILLER, author of *The Coast of Akron*

"Charlie Martens is my favorite kind of narrator, an obsessive yearner whose commitment to his worldview is so overwhelming that the distance between his words and the reader's usual thinking gets clouded fast. *World Gone Water* will draw you in, make you complicit, and finally leave you both discomfited and thrilled."

—MATT BELL, author of
In the House upon the Dirt between the Lake and the Woods

10651303

World Gone Water

Westfield Memorial Library
Westfield, New Jersey

World Gone Water

A NOVEL

Jaime Clarke

Roundabout Press   2015

Copyright © 2015 by Jaime Clarke

All rights reserved. This is a work of fiction. Names, characters, places, and incidents either are the products of the author's imagination or are used fictitiously. Any resemblance to actual events, locales, or persons, living or dead, is entirely coincidental.

Roundabout Press
PO Box 370310
West Hartford, CT 06137

ISBN: 978-0985881283

Printed in the United States of America

10   9   8   7   6   5   4   3   2   1

FIRST EDITION

For my son—

and for yours

And if everything is so nebulous about a matter so elementary as the morals of sex, what is there to guide us in the more subtle morality of all other personal contacts, associations, and activities? Or are we meant to act on impulse alone?

—Ford Madox Ford, *The Good Soldier*

World Gone Water

Sonoran Rehabilitation Center Entrance Essay

Why I'm Here
Charlie Martens

I am not a good person. I don't need anyone to tell me that I am not a model citizen. People can always improve and I want to be a better person. I want what better people have. In my own defense, though, I do have moments when I reach up and brush my fingers on the brass ring of kindness, charity, and compassion.

In further defense of myself, I have to say that I am principally proud of who I am, proud that I have navigated so well with what some have called a faulty compass. Before anyone in here judges me, or starts an intense investigation into who I am, first you have to come to grips with the following ten ideas:

1. I am not a son of privilege, yet I am not an orphan of poverty.
2. I do not hold degrees from institutions of higher learning.
3. I am not handsome enough to operate on looks alone.
4. I have no family traditions.
5. I have the same dreams everyone else has, dreams whose origins are in the common myths of our time.

6. I am easygoing but will sometimes tend toward violence, if
   provoked.
7. I believe in equality.
8. I am a protector of those things in life that are smaller and
   weaker than I am.
9. I can't stand ignorance, idiocy, or intolerant behavior.
10. People talk about me in terms of sweetness and charm.

I don't pretend that these ten ideas define me, but they help you get a better view from where you are, looking down on me. The view from here is not one of looking up, I assure you, but merely looking out.

An eleventh idea is that I do not judge people.

If you want to know how far I've come, you have to understand what I've overcome. I don't just see things, I *feel* them. You can blame a fascination with appearance and how things seem on any modern thing you like. I did. But I didn't find any answers in blame, and maybe the only truth I know is this: You have to feel something to understand it.

You ask me why I'm here, and I'll tell you that I'm here to feel my way further into the world. I haven't been remanded to your custody. I simply took Detective Rodriguez's advice. Your only job is not to judge me based on what you see.

Exit Interview Report

I, Jane Ramsey, in my capacity as a clinical psychologist employed by Sonoran Rehabilitation Center, located in Maricopa County, Arizona, do hereby swear that this exit interview report contains my personal evaluation of Charlie Martens. This exit interview is being conducted after the completion of Mr. Martens's voluntary nine-month stay.

STATEMENT OF FACTS: Mr. Martens was a person of interest in a sexual assault investigation in the state of Florida, though he was never charged due to the unreliability and ultimate disappearance of the accuser. On the recommendation of Detective Florio Rodriguez of the Boca Raton Police Department, Mr. Martens enrolled in SRC. Upon his successful treatment, Jay Stanton Buckley has guaranteed Mr. Martens's position as a functioning member of society, gainfully employed by Buckley Cosmetics in a public relations capacity.

TREATMENT: Mr. Martens participated in every aspect of SRC's program. His monthly journal entries and essay assignments are appended herewith. At Mr. Martens's request, his creative writing exercises have not been admitted to the record.

OBSERVATIONS: Mr. Martens's rehabilitation at SRC has been a concentrated effort to even out his mind about the opposite sex and relations with women. An unexplained, alternating inborn hostility and passivity toward women has, in my opinion, been leveled, and a truer, more mature personality has been erected in its place. During his stay at SRC, Mr. Martens has displayed mannerly and cordial behavior toward the women here, both on staff and inpatient alike. Personally I find Mr. Martens a pleasant and charming individual. His presence in group and on the campus here shall be missed.

The following is a complete record and true account of Mr. Martens's rehabilitation.

Signed and dated this day——

-- Jane

If you ask me about Jane, I'll tell you that she is a fine woman. It is true that in the catalog of women in my life, Jane would come under *P* for "plain," but she is tender and we go together pretty good. Besides, I prefer not to make aesthetic judgments.

The thing I like most about Jane is that she looks best without makeup. On one of our first dates, right after I left SRC, Jane had put on bright red lipstick, and the whole night I tried not to stare at it, because it looked like she was smiling even when she wasn't, and by the end of the night I was self-conscious about it. I think she sensed I didn't like it, or maybe she was uncomfortable with it too. Jane has never worn lipstick again.

We keep each other at arm's length most of the time and that is really for the best. (She knows it too.) I guess one could say our relationship is not complicated by love. We are, however, into each other totally. Our relationship is utopian. Utopian relationships last longer than marriages because emotions like jealousy and envy are removed. I never think about anyone but Jane, and Jane always tells me I'm the one for her. It wouldn't be fair if it weren't that way, and it is the only real promise we've made.

It wasn't always like that, though. At first, Jane thought I was dangerous. She didn't say much , but she warmed up when I showed her what a nice guy I can be. Jane said she'd come off a relationship with a fellow who had probably once been in prison. You have to take the good from your last relationship and put it in future ones, I told her.

And that's what we did, creating our present utopian relationship, which provides her with whatever it is she wants. This is the sort of relationship a woman like Jane deserves. It is the sort of relationship I like to initiate.

If I could change one thing about Jane, though, I wouldn't make her such a big Christian. I don't have a problem with religion per se, but sometimes Jane can really confuse the issue. Besides, like I've told her over and over again, there is no religion in Utopia.

But then, Jane thinks I am the Antichrist. "You're the devil," she is always telling me. If she says it too often, I start to get a pinched feeling in my head and I have to yell at her to stop. I won't yell at her in public, though, and I never take it out on her in bed.

Jane is moving to California, but I want her to stay. I make a point to say "California is *not* Utopia" at least once a day, just slipping it into a conversation casually. Jane raises her eyebrows and shrugs in a way that lets me know she is on the fence. I'm convinced I can get her to stay.

"What's in California?" I ask her.

"You could come with me," she answers. She knows from my sessions with Dr. Hatch that because my parents were killed when we lived in California, it's a blank spot on my mental map. Even my short stay with my aunt and uncle in San Diego feels like it took place out of time, and out of country. Of my own will, I will never return to California, a fact Jane knows well.

"But I don't want to move to California."

"Charlie, you could easily come."

"But I don't want to," I repeat, and this signals Jane that I don't want to discuss it.

So I'm in the mood for a good time, and Jane and I are getting ready at her apartment to go out for the usual—dinner and whatever. She sees that I am on the verge of what could almost pass as euphoria, and I see that look on her face that lets me know it won't be smooth sailing.

And sure enough on the way to dinner Jane gets me uptight by demanding to know the name of the restaurant. When I don't tell her—when I say that I want it to be a surprise—she pursues the question about what kind of food this restaurant serves with an irrationality that becomes so frightening I finally do tell her, and though I'm disappointed about the deletion of the only mystery the evening holds, I'm glad this has happened, that the glitch is out of the system, that I can now breathe easy through dinner.

Sometimes I think I would like to marry Jane, but I know that our relationship couldn't survive the rules and constraints of a formal institution like marriage. Still, she carries herself in such a way that someone across the room looking at her would think, *Hey, that girl crossing the room could make a pretty good wife.* Someday someone should marry Jane and I'm pretty sure someday someone will.

Depending on Jane's mood after dinner, we will either go to the Sugar Bowl for ice cream or go straight back to her place. I always hope we will go for ice cream because I like to watch Jane coo like a little girl between licks of mint chocolate chip. Not only is it an amazing transformation, but it always signals the start of at least an hour of foreplay that lasts all the way from the Sugar Bowl to her bed.

Tonight dinner clearly makes Jane pensive, and I can sense that she won't want mint chocolate chip and indeed the whole rest of the night may be in jeopardy. I dread the thought of going back to my room at the Hotel San Carlos, my temporary encampment courtesy of Buckley Cosmetics, alone. The historic boutique hotel is situated in a part of downtown I hardly know at all, and when I return to my room, I have to pretend that I'm just a tourist to stave off the depression brought on by my small pink room. Regardless of Jane's mood, her apartment is always preferable to another night in the hotel.

"I'm going to California," she says, as if trying to cheer herself up.

"I'll go with you," I say, and wait for her reaction. The skin under her eyes tightens, confirming my suspicion that she doesn't really want me to.

"I thought you wanted to stay here." She tries to act like she hasn't been caught off guard.

"I could stay or I could go," I tell her, shrugging.

"Well, *I'm* going," she says, realizing I am toying with her. My coyness cheers her up and again I am sure I can convince her to stay.

As the result of a bet I lost concerning how long I could pleasure Jane in bed (although I was just seven minutes shy of the promised thirty minutes, which, Jane assured me, was only average), I have to go to church with her every Sunday this month.

"If you can prove you're omnipotent, you don't have to go," she teased. But, of course, I am not.

Jane being the Catholic she is, we sit in one of the back pews, like I used to at mandatory Mass at Randolph Prep, in the Gallery of Heathens. When Mr. Chandler, my guardian's neighbor, used his pull as an alum to help me transfer to Randolph, he didn't mention that it was an all-boys Catholic school, though it hardly mattered. I was all but finished at the public school where his foster daughter Talie went.

The priests march in an impressive parade, dressed in black and red garb, holding long staffs with banners that could have been made during the Crusades, and the head priest—the Pontifex Maximus, the one leading the way—bows prayerfully from side to side.

The entourage halts in front of the congregation, and the priests assemble in an indeterminate order behind a long counter on a stage.

I look over at Jane, who knows I am about to say something snide and ignores me.

The magic act begins with a bowl on the table belching white powder, and I crane my neck to get a better glimpse. One of the elderly priests on the left of the Pontifex Maximus, dangling a charm on the end of a gold chain, begins swinging the chain back and forth, the audience mesmerized. Some sort of liquid is poured into the bowl and now suddenly all of the priests are busy with their hands, and in my mind I superimpose the title *Cooking with Catholics* over the whole scene. I lean over to share this with Jane, but she leans away from me.

After an inordinate amount of standing and sitting, singing and muttering, standing and sitting, I feel the end is near. Anxiety washes over me as I anticipate the benediction, like the anxiety a smoker in a business meeting feels when he senses he will finally get to step outside for a cigarette. There is an unquiet silence and those in the very front pew stand . I groan to myself and fold my hands on the pew in front of me and rest my head in the empty triangle they form. The shuffle of feet and the murmuring of the Eucharist become a drone in my ears as I close my eyes, wondering what I would pray about if I prayed.

I imagine Jane on her knees, at the foot of her bed. Is she praying that we'll get married? Or is she praying for things only for herself—her family's wellness, or for the right decision about California?

Without warning, an image of Jane and her next boyfriend praying together, heads down, hands together, appears in my mind. The suddenness of seeing them quickens my pulse and a bitter irritability creeps through me. The image is static and overpowering, like a giant poster plastered on the wall of my brain, and the thought occurs to me that Jane probably *will* pray for me, given her good, religious nature. Privately she asks the Lord to watch over me and protect me from evil. This thought stays with me until we are out in the parking lot, and as we climb into Jane's car, I say, "Fuck church."

"You're the devil," Jane says.

Essay #1: A Proper Introduction

Before I was anything, I was an Elrod Bullet.

Ms. Saltonstall, my second-grade teacher at Elrod, told me I was her favorite. I was her helper because I held the spoon full of sugar while she held the flame under it during science, because I read longer passages than anyone else during English, because in math I didn't have to go to the board, since Ms. Saltonstall knew I hated it. The girls in my class noticed this and began to believe that I was special too. Whatever I didn't know then, I felt some sort of special force working in my favor—to the exclusion of all the other boys in my class, and it made me a king.

My main group of friends—Wendy, Ronda, Cheryl, and Sally Ann—and I were always together. We would hang off the monkey bars and squeal, or see who could swing higher on the swing set. These girls liked to match whatever I did. If I jumped out of the swing, they'd try to jump farther.

Sometimes Wendy and Ronda went to Cheryl's house, or Cheryl and Wendy would go to Ronda's house, or Cheryl and Ronda went to Wendy's house, or they would all go to Sally Ann's, but I never went to any of their houses. They would invite me, but my grandmother wouldn't let me go. I invited them over once, but when my grandmother found the five of us in my room playing a game of Sorry! in our bathing suits, she called their mothers, who said they'd assumed my mother was home when they granted permission for the girls to join me for afternoon snacks. I taught the girls a new phrase, "Never assume. It makes an ass out of you and me," and we laughed about that until Wendy and Ronda and Cheryl and Sally Ann said they didn't want to play with me anymore.

On the last day of school there was a field trip to the Denver Observatory. Even though it was daytime, we were staring at stars through a giant telescope. "How can there be stars?" Wendy asked. None of us understood it, or heard an answer.

If I ever see Wendy or Ronda or Cheryl or Sally Ann—which seems doubtful now; they appear not real but as ghosts in my mind—I'll tell them what I know: that if you really look, you can see what others can't.

Most Likely To

My then-best-friend-now-ex-best-friend Jason handles it real cool. He was our high school's master thespian.

"How much each?" he negotiates with the one in the faded Michael Jackson *Thriller* T-shirt.

"Are you cops?" she asks, reaching inside the passenger window. She gives my soft crotch a squeeze.

"We're not cops," I say. I was against this at first, on principle, but Thriller's touch is warm and I can feel the wheels in motion. Suddenly I'm gung ho.

"I get thirty dollars," she says. That leaves me with the pregnant one, who turns out to be more expensive, fifty bucks.

Thriller tells us to circle the block, and we take out all our money, counting out what we need, putting the rest in the glove box. When we get them in our headlights again, the pregnant one is pointing toward the alley.

"Just stay relaxed," the master thespian says. "But keep your eyes open."

Jason's car reeks of his girlfriend's perfume, even though it's been more than an hour since we dropped Sara off, right after we dropped off Jane. Jason and I have sought out common ground with these hookers; it's where we left off, what we used to do when we were both transfer students at Randolph Prep, outsiders in an exclusive club. Bumping into Jason in the cereal aisle at an Albertsons, it was like yesterday we threw that cup of warm piss on that guy riding his bike home late, or the time we climbed in the fountain at City Hall, stripping and shitting until we had good-size pieces we could pitch. "Hey, batter, batter. He can't hit, he can't hit, he can't hit, *swing* batter."

Sure, I felt the old stuff, too. Our jealous rivalry, kept alive in high school more by him than by me, a rivalry that faded the summer of our junior year, when I was selected for a prestigious summer fellowship and he wasn't. The way he produced Sara as evidence that he had the perfect relationship. I introduced him to Jane too, and I could see in his eyes that he was anxious to size me up, see who's who.

Thriller and Preggers wave for us to pull in, dancing impatiently in the headlights.

"What should we do?" I ask.

Jason is watching the two hookers, studying them. In situations like these, his mind is a steel trap. "I'm going to give them a scare."

He flips the headlights out. Thriller and Preggers disappear into the dark and Jason rolls down his window, yelling "Fucking whores" as he pushes the accelerator to the floor, plunging toward the streetlight at the end of the alley.

Jason knows about what happened to me, and I appreciate the way he treats me like it was just yesterday we were two transfer students at Randolph, him from New York and me from nowhere. It's a good friend who will overlook what other people think about you.

Aztecka

Jason's bar, Aztecka, is packed, the strobes lighting the massive movement of people on the dance floor. I cross Camelback Road and walk up to the door. An ultra-yuppie couple appears, their noses turned up at the industrialites crowding the dance floor, desecrating their mahogany and green plush carpet. "All I wanted was a kiwi margarita," the woman says.

It isn't really Jason's bar. He's the manager, and since I've been back, I've been helping him out on the busy nights.

I've always thought the best part of working in a bar, obviously enough, would be meeting women.

The worst part is seeing what people do to each other. A bar is the perfect environment to do real harm to someone you don't really know.

Miles, the relief bartender, hands me an apron and we face the throng at the bar, two deep. It still takes me a minute to orient myself, but once I do, I feel like I never left La Onda, the bar I tended in Boca Raton, where I went to escape memories of Jenny and ended up finding Karine.

I'm making four or five drinks at once while having two or three more orders shouted at me, and suddenly I hear a *whack* and then

it seems like everyone freezes and I see this guy and this girl and
the girl is holding the side of her face and she's begging him not
to leave her there and that's when I notice another girl waiting off
to the side, impatiently, and the first girl is in tears, blubbering. I
hear the guy say, "If *you* won't do it, *she* will." I look over at the girl
to see if she really will, and our gazes lock and I can't make myself
look away. The first girl's pleading becomes pathetic and she starts
convulsing; her voice crescendoes and everyone is listening but the
guy doesn't realize it and he smacks her across the face again. I
start in the direction of the guy and he faces me, scowling. The
showdown. I reach under the bar, go for an invisible bat, and he
sees this and grabs the girl-in-waiting and cuts through the crowd
to the door.

There's a hum and then the bar is at 140 decibels, the noise
swallowing the girlfriend who is left standing in the corner, holding
her face. People are screaming for their drinks, but I ignore them
and call out to the girl. I wave a drunk guy off his stool and motion
for her to sit.

"Are you okay?" I ask.

Clearly embarrassed, she just nods.

"What was that all about?" I ask.

"Can I have a drink?" she asks.

"Sure. What do you want?"

"Just water."

I hand her a glass of water and she takes a sip and sets it back
down on the bar.

"Want to talk about it?" I ask, feeling like I can really help her,
but she just shakes her head and asks me to call her a cab.

When the cab arrives, I search the bar for her, and just as I'm
about to shrug at the cabdriver waiting in the doorway, the girl
emerges from the bathroom. I wave, trying to get her attention,

but she isn't looking at me. Instead she turns away and heads to the pool room in back. I signal the cabdriver to stay where he is, and go after her.

I find the girl leaning against one of the pool tables, and when I walk up to her, she gets a strange look on her face like she wonders who I am. Her boyfriend is back and he comes up to me. "What do you want?" he asks, sneering.

"Your cab is here," I say to the girl.

"I don't need it," she says, turning away.

"The driver's waiting out front," I tell her, trying to persuade her to go home, where she'll be safe.

"Look, I already said I didn't want it. Are you deaf?" She scowls at me, and now her boyfriend moves in closer and I consider throwing him out, but I begin to feel a shift in loyalties on the girl's part and I turn and start to walk away. A hand grabs my arm and I whirl around, ready to deck the asshole, but it's the girl and she asks me: "Do you know where we can score some smack?"

I'm still hearing the girl's question when I'm back behind the bar, not so much the words, but how she asked it. Sometimes you can mistake unhappiness for despair.

Jane gets me into helping people and it turns out I'm a natural. The first deal didn't turn out so well: I guess I'm not great with children.

I had been volunteering with Jane at the crisis nursery for only about a week when I hurt someone (it was an accident). I was playing along fine with the kids, running around and screaming, in and out of the miniature wood house, an old set piece from some play, donated by a local theater company. I had chased some kids into the house, ducking into the tiny front room, where the kids were pressed one on top of the other in the corner. I pretended like I was going to really get them, and this little Mexican kid started kicking me in the leg. I yelled at him to stop, which made the kids laugh, and this little Mexican kid kept doing it until I put my hand on his head and pushed him back against the wall.

Of course there was a big stink about who did what. The little Mexican kid accused me of hitting him. I said the little Mexican kid fell. I said I was sorry about it. I said I felt bad. I think they believed me, but I didn't get to help out at the nursery anymore.

I told Jane this story (minus what I did to the Mexican kid), and she suggested I volunteer for the March of Dimes Bowl-A-Rama, which turned out to be a right-on suggestion.

"Thanks for coming," Katherine said.

"Glad to help out," I said grandly.

"We've got several volunteers for today," Katherine said. "If you like it, maybe you'll think about staying on."

"Sure," I said. "We'll see."

I was assigned to a girl named Janice. Janice couldn't talk very well and walked like she might pitch forward or backward, depending on how you looked at her. And she couldn't stop smiling.

Janice seemed to like me right away, and I helped her with her bowling. The March of Dimes had these special ramps set up in front of the lanes that looked like slides at the water park.

"Like this," I said, showing Janice how to put her fingers in the holes and lift the ball up onto the ramp. Janice watched the ball roll down, picking up speed, until it thumped in the lane and slowly rolled toward the pins.

Janice clapped wildly as the ball veered into the gutter, grounding past the upright pins.

"You try it," I suggested, and she said something unintelligible. She lifted the ball with both hands and loaded it onto the ramp. "Like this," she said.

"Good job, Janice," I said. Her ball guttered, and we both stood wondering what to do next.

"Watch," I said, pushing the ramp to the side. I took up a ball and let it fly down the lane.

"Wheeeeee!" Janice screamed. Everyone looked over, and I thought for a minute I might get into trouble, but the sound of the pins crashing into one another brought cheers and applause from the others, and I just smiled blankly at everyone.

"Are you my brother?" Janice asked.

"What's that?" I asked.

"You're my brother," she said.

I didn't know what to do, and Janice started pawing at me in a surprisingly lewd manner. I stepped back and Katherine rushed up.

"Sorry," Katherine said. "She thinks all men are her brother."

"Oh," I said.

Janice ignored us and picked up another bowling ball, peering into it as if it were a mirror.

"Where is her brother?" I asked hesitantly.

"He's in jail," Katherine said.

"Really?"

"He molested her."

I nodded my head like I understood, because I didn't really know what else to do. The information didn't mean anything to me—I had just met Janice and I didn't know her brother and I was pretty sure her brother's molesting her hadn't made Janice handicapped. Mostly I felt like I couldn't really do anything for Janice even though I knew this about her.

I was sulking about what a crappy person I probably was when Katherine said, "She thinks all men are her brother, so she thinks it's okay for all men to do to her what her brother did."

Janice began dropping balls right onto the lane, one after another, clapping madly at their dull thumps.

Katherine lunged to stop her.

I thought about men taking advantage of Janice.

I wondered if *I* would.

I wondered if I knew anyone who would.

I could picture several.

Essay #2: I Touch Clouds

All the boys in high school thought my neighbor Talie was pretty, and they all tried to get dates with her. She wasn't as pretty as some of the cheerleaders, but those girls only had what you saw. With Talie, boys knew she felt things most girls didn't, and they wanted to feel them too.

Talie had natural grace. When I wanted to learn how to dance for the Christmas formal, Talie volunteered to help. We would practice in her foster parents' living room, the coffee table standing awkwardly on its end, pushed in the corner to make more space. We pretended we were at a grand ball, hooking up arm in arm in the kitchen doorway, entering the room stride for stride and turning to each other. I bowed and she curtsied.

"Not too fast," Mrs. Chandler, her foster mother, would say, marking the time by slapping her hand against her leg.

Talie moved majestically and I tried to follow, becoming lost in the way she looked directly into my eyes before she dipped me. My head went right for the floor until I thought I would bring us both down, but her arm would catch, saving me, bringing me back up, making me look graceful too. Talie would spin me out, away from her, and I would rotate like a satellite, pulled back in by her gravity.

**

"Not too fast," Talie said. "You're hurting me."

I eased up.

"Don't stop," she said. "Just don't go so fast."

I remember the pain and fear I would feel when I would come while masturbating, but with Talie, things felt different. Her breath was warm and touching her was like running your fingers along clouds.

"Doesn't it feel good?" she would ask.

"I'm going to come," I said, warning her.

"Shit," she said, stopping suddenly. "I don't want to get pregnant."

Talie climbed off and lay on her side, facing me. I felt her fingers on me, moving back and forth, and I did the same for her. We came out of sync, me first, then her. She cupped her hand to keep me from making a mess on the sheets. I watched her lean over the sink in the bathroom as she scrubbed her hands.

Most of the time she would just come over and ask me to. We wouldn't kiss on the mouth or anything corny like that. She would just say she wanted to, and I don't think there was ever a time when I didn't want to. I'd just ask if the coast was clear, and she would nod and lock the door.

"You're learning," Mrs. Chandler said.

It didn't matter that no one at the formal would dance.

I was glad.

I didn't want to show anyone what Talie had shown me.

From the Deep End

Jason wants to come in and say hi, but I tell him it's better if he drops me at the front gate. "I haven't seen JSB in forever," he says.

"Maybe next time," I say, and he gets it.

I wait until Jason is out of sight to punch in my gate code. I'm surprised that it still works and the heavy metal gate rolls back on its track, retracting behind the concrete walls of Arrowhead Ranch.

The red Land Cruiser that JSB is going to loan me is parked in the far corner of the driveway. If I could jump into the Land Cruiser and drive away, I would.

Heading up the back walkway, I kick through an overgrown row of birds of paradise, their orangish flowers drooping and rotting. The upright arm of the giant saguaro outside the back kitchen window has rotted too, and it rests elbow-out at the top of the walkway. Weeds sprout up through the graveled cactus beds underneath the picture windows.

I knock on the back door. Through the kitchen window I see a pizza box next to an empty plastic pitcher of iced tea on the cutting block in the middle of the kitchen. I consider going around to the front, to where the bell is, but knock again, harder, until JSB shuffles into the kitchen, sees me, and smiles.

He opens the door with considerable effort, and a stiff foulness rises to my nose when he opens his arms, a smile somewhere deep within him barely visible on his face.

"When?" he asks.

"While you were in Canada," I say apologetically.

JSB nods. "Was there any trouble there?" he asks.

I shake my head no. "They were fine," I say.

"I told them to call me if there was—"

"There wasn't," I say.

We sit at the rattan kitchen table, and JSB reaches for an invisible glass, looks back toward the refrigerator and then at me, leaning comfortably in his chair.

"Did Talie tell you?" he asks.

"That you fired your landscapers?" I ask, smiling.

JSB glances out the window and snorts. "Buckley Cosmetics is going to file for bankruptcy," he tells me.

I lean back in my chair, stunned. I know so little about the world that I didn't know it was possible for a company to file for bankruptcy twice in its corporate life. The trauma of the previous bankruptcy, when I first came to work for JSB and Buckley, was easily summoned.

"We're so far in the red we need the protection," he says matter-of-factly. "We were hoping the new line of cosmetics would save us, but the development has been delayed by at least six months and the banks won't cooperate anymore."

"Can't you take a personal loan?" I ask. I can't remember when I'd last offered advice to anyone. For the first time in a long time I feel like I am really helping someone.

"My credit lines are overextended," he says, shrugging.

I'm turning it over, trying to come up with the solution, when there's laughter on the walkway. I look out the window, but JSB sits

still in his chair, not turning when the door opens and a woman—a
girl, really—who looks like Victoria, JSB's girlfriend when I left for
Boca Raton, blond and honey-kissed, but who is not Victoria, saunters
in with an embarrassed dark-haired kid no more than eighteen in
tow. "Hi," she says, kissing JSB lightly on his graying hair.

JSB smiles and fingers the pepper shaker on the table.

"We want to use the pool," the girl says. "Is that all right?"

"Sure," JSB says. "Help yourself."

The two disappear as quickly as they arrived, and JSB gets up,
motioning for me to follow.

"Thanks for loaning me the vehicle," I say.

We're in front of the smoked-glass picture window overlooking
the pool. JSB drags over a couple of chairs and we sit.

"What's her name?" I ask.

"Erin," JSB answers.

"How long have you been seeing her?"

"Six months," he says, sighing.

If a woman in JSB's life lasts six months, it's like ten years in
a regular relationship. The six-month anniversary at Arrowhead
Ranch usually calls for a locksmith and a reprogramming of the
front gate.

"Where is Talie?" I ask, looking toward the end of the house, in
the direction of her bedroom.

"I haven't seen her," JSB says, not taking his eyes off the pool,
where Erin and Erin's friend are pushing a volleyball back and forth
across the water's surface. "I've been thinking of making Erin . . .
permanent."

"Really?" I'm as surprised as I was when JSB called from
Atlanta when I was seventeen, freshly emancipated, working for
JSB as a corporate runner for Buckley Cosmetics—a job Talie
helped me get—and told me he was engaged to his high school

sweetheart, whom he'd met up with again. By the time his plane landed in Phoenix a week later, there was no mention of the high school sweetheart, and the whole episode remains an aberrant dream among the very real personalities of the women he's been with before and since.

"The secret is to let them think they're going to get a piece of everything," JSB used to tell me. "By the time they figure it out, you're ready for the next one." This advice resurfaced in my mind now and again because it was an unusually calculated thing to say, especially coming from a man who so passionately believed in romance. This advice was repeated with a frequency that suggested it was a joke, something he'd picked up from someone who'd said it, or half said it, or was making a joke too.

Erin and her friend are sitting on the steps in the shallow end, leaning back on their elbows. They collapse in laughter and Erin puts her head on the boy's chest. The boy buries his nose in Erin's wet hair and JSB puts his hand up to the glass window.

"I should probably go," I say, wondering where Talie is.

JSB awakens from his trance. "The keys are on the counter," he says. He pats my knee and smiles.

I nod and he turns his gaze back toward the pool, not able to look away from what shines in front of him.

Essay #3: An Ideal Day Sometime in the Near Future

This is an ideal day sometime in the near future:

I meet someone who can appreciate me for what I can offer and we spend a lot of time together. But we don't get trapped by love. We just like being together and we realize that it isn't forever, that eventually we'll move on, but that we'll always remember what we had with each other.

And after that relationship is over, I meet someone else who can appreciate me for what I can offer, etc.

-- Tuesday

Tuesdays, Jane volunteers at the crisis nursery, and Tuesdays put Jane in a good mood. We both always look forward to Tuesday nights, and this Tuesday night seems especially good because afterward, our backs against the crumpled sheets, we solidify the Utopian Love Code:

"If a man makes promises to a woman and does not keep his promises, another man shall fulfill the obligation," I start. "If a man has stolen another man's woman, and if that woman was unhappy, that woman shall remain with the man; however, if the woman is said to have been happy, she shall be returned to the man from whom she was stolen."

This makes Jane giggle and she adds: "If a man has put a spell upon a woman, and has not justified himself, the man shall plunge into the holy river, and if the holy river overcomes him, his intentions are bad; but if the holy river bears him out and shows him innocent, his intentions are good and he may proceed with his sorcery."

"If a fire breaks out in a woman's heart and a man extinguishes the fire, he shall be set fire himself."

"If a man has married a wife and has not made her feelings and her property part of a whole, she is no wife."

"If a woman's reputation is besmirched by another male without just cause, he shall throw himself into the holy river for the sake of the purity of Utopia."

Jane props herself up on her elbow and adds: "A woman's feelings cannot be hurt, taken for granted, abused, or ridiculed."

I frown at this and tell her that the rule about besmirched reputations covers this, and she just stares at me and then rolls away, and I guess we've pretty much covered the basic tenets, but I review them silently for oversights.

Journal #1

Their days always appear to me this way:

Jenny saunters through the house, opening the curtains, everything in full view. As always, she boils water in the microwave for her morning oatmeal—maple and brown sugar. Gray light pours in as she sits at the table in a white terry-cloth robe, a purple satin nightgown peeking out. After she tilts the bowl and scrapes it twice with her spoon, Jenny rinses it in the sink and walks back to her bedroom, which is on the far side of the house. When Jenny reappears, she is dressed for her job teaching first grade at the elementary school in town.

And when school lets out, Jenny drives home, stopping by the market, browsing through the aisles, wandering back and forth across the store, then, realizing the time, she hurriedly fills a basket.

Ben pulls up as Jenny is unloading the groceries, and he kisses her on the cheek before lifting a paper bag from the station wagon, slipping on the shoveled driveway, catching himself as the bag hits the ground. He picks it up again, pretending nothing has happened.

My stomach turns when I think of Ben—weak, not a challenger, not a contender, kept in only by her will—who is unable to understand Jenny the way I did.

She loves me. She loves me not. She loves me. She loves me not. She loves me but doesn't know that I still love her, more than anyone in the world, and I see the light in the living room go out, the house dark for a moment, Jenny sitting on the edge of the bed, Jenny smiling when Ben walks in and closes their bedroom door and kisses her on the forehead before he draws the blinds.

I imagine me at their wedding (even though I wasn't invited): The redbrick church appears to be receding into the pale summer sky, purely an optical illusion brought on by the sun and the whiskey sours I drank earlier, and I wonder if anyone in the church can see me, down the street, hidden behind the drooping oleanders.

I unbutton the vest of my suit and check my hair in the mirror on the visor. The last invited guest arrived ten minutes ago, and I am debating how I will make my entrance: before or after the ceremony? I can imagine the look on Jenny's face, everyone staring at me, bewildered. I fondle the dozen red roses I've been keeping cool in my refrigerator. The street is empty and I stare hard at a lone palm tree swaying back and forth, obscuring part of the church steeple, fanning the heat back toward the shimmering yellow sun.

The doors of the church swing wide and Jenny's uncle appears, walking hurriedly to his van, not fifty feet from where I am. The van door groans deeply, echoing in my head, and he lifts out his camera bag. I slide down in my seat, and as Jenny's uncle slams the van door, he recognizes my car. A sweat breaks out on my forehead while he stares, trying to see past the window tint, and he takes a step toward me. I reach down for the gear shift, my hand quivering, and slowly press in the clutch. He sets his camera bag on the neatly manicured lawn, looks both ways, and crosses the street toward me, shaking his head. I feel my body convulse as I pop the car in gear, lurching forward, spilling the roses around my feet, barreling down the street, crying.

**

Junior year, when my focus should've been on my new classmates at Randolph Prep, I met and fell in love with Jenny, a freshman saxophone player at a public school on the west side of Phoenix. Mr. Chandler had given me a saxophone abandoned by one of his foster kids, suggesting that I join band at Randolph as a means of making friends quickly. I knew firsthand that transfer students were easily made pariahs and followed his advice; Jason knew too, which is why he signed up for theater the first day of classes.

The randomness of Jenny and me sitting together on the bus ferrying selected students to the statewide marching competition was not random at all: The months of Saturday practices on the empty fields of Scottsdale Community College had provided hours of close infantry training. The trip to Northern Arizona University in Flagstaff, the competition venue, was merely the culmination. Jenny and I sat together on the two-hour trip, flirting. As we neared Flagstaff, I nervously popped my saxophone reed into my mouth, claiming to have to moisten it before the competition. "Try to bite it," I said playfully, sticking the small reed out like a tiny wooden tongue. I pulled back as Jenny shyly inched forward and snapped at the reed like a guppy. "Try again," I said. This time I didn't pull back, watching as she zoomed toward me, her green eyes sparkling. She bit the reed and held it, finally releasing it. "Again," I said softly, this time dropping the reed in my lap as she leaned in, kissing her, the spark of our long-suffering flirting a danger to the pine trees that whisked past us as the bus entered the Flagstaff city limits.

"She's a Mormon, dude," someone said when I confirmed my interest.

I shrugged, unsure of what that meant.

From that time forward, Jenny and I were inseparable. I quickly assimilated into her circle of friends, who were exclusively Mormon.

The Mormon kids at her school were not a small population and were generally good students and well liked, and I found their approval and acceptance easier than that of the rich kids at Randolph. Jenny's family was a first-generation conversion (someone her father worked with had convinced them to convert), and when, upon meeting me, her mother asked her in front of me if I was LDS, I had no idea what that meant. Jenny answered that I wasn't and I let the matter drop, my happiness at being with Jenny blocking out the white noise around me. Her parents wouldn't allow us to officially date until Jenny turned sixteen, so our courtship took place entirely at her house after school. The matter of where I lived never arose, and it was some time before it surfaced that my birth parents were dead and that I'd been shunted from distant relative to distant relative before landing in Phoenix at the home of my first cousin twice removed. That I attended an all-boys Catholic school didn't seem to register with them, and I hid from them the fact that I'd recently been legally emancipated.

Still, the ease and speed with which our relationship grew serious might've been alarming to Jenny's parents, but their recent separation consumed them, and Jenny and I were essentially left alone, free to wander her family's property, an unworked farm outside of Phoenix, a parcel among parcels in what was primarily farmland. We rode the family three-wheeler back and forth to visit her cousin, who lived on an adjoining parcel; sometimes we took her horse, who spooked me. Usually we watched television or listened to music while we shot pool in her living room, her pool skills far superior to mine. I was always aware that her mother was lurking around the house, though, maybe looking out a window, or listening for the quiet that portends making out. Her home was a sanctuary that offered us a place out of time in which to get to know each other. That she had never seen my house (her mother forbade her) or that we didn't hang out with my friends (a small population, but still) was not a concern. We did manage outside dates of a sort: Every so often a couple of Mormon stakes (each church or ward was part of a stake; Jenny belonged to the Tolsun ward, which in turn belonged to the West Maricopa stake) got together and hosted a dance.

Anyone could participate in the dances, regardless of religion; however, before attending your first dance, you had to acquire a dance card from the local bishop. I made the requisite appointment. The bishop, an older man with prematurely skeletal features, welcomed me and asked me into his spartan office. We exchanged a few pleasantries—I told him about how Jenny was my girlfriend and ran down the roster of my friends who attended the Tolsun ward—and then settled into business. The bishop handed me a small yellow piece of paper, the dance card I'd come for, invalid without the bishop's signature, which he was happy to sign after I read and consented to the rules on the back of the card:

1. Ages 14–18
2. Valid dance card must be presented at the door for admission. (We will accept valid dance cards from other stakes.) Replacement charge for lost card is $5.00.
3. The Word of Wisdom to be observed: No tobacco, alcohol, or drugs are permitted inside the building or on the premises.
4. BOYS shall wear dress pants (no Levi's, jeans, denims, or imitations of any color, or other non–dress pants). Shirts must have collars. No sandals are allowed. (Nice tennis shoes are OK.) Socks must be worn with shoes. No hats, earrings, or gloves.
5. GIRLS shall not wear tight-fitting dresses or skirts or have bare shoulders (blouses and dresses must have sleeves). Hemlines of dresses are to be of modest length (to the knee). No dresses or skirts with slits or cuts above the knee.

6. After admittance to the dance, you are to remain inside the building.
7. No loitering or sitting in cars on church grounds.
8. Automobiles shall be driven in a quiet and courteous manner, so as not to disturb the residents in the area.
9. No acrobatics, bear-hugging, bumping, rolling on floor, or exhibitions.
10. Personal conduct and behavior shall be that expected from exemplary young ladies and gentlemen.

"Can you agree to these rules?" the bishop asked.

I said that I could.

"Very good," he said, taking the slip of paper from me and laboriously signing his name to it. "Have you considered joining our church?" he asked as he handed my dance card back.

I hadn't. "I might," I said, knowing that was the answer he wanted to hear. He regarded me cautiously.

"You might attend with Jenny and her family," the bishop said. I wondered if he knew about Jenny's parents' marital status, guessing that he didn't. The topic was never broached in Jenny's house, or in her cousin's house, everyone pretending like the fact that Jenny's mother and father were still married but not living in the same house was as natural as their counterparts living together.

The next question caught me off guard. "Have you and Jenny been intimate?"

I couldn't tell if the bishop was joking or not, so I laughed, suppressing a sickening feeling that was building in my stomach. I answered no automatically, not just because it was the truth but because I hoped the answer would stifle the look of surprise on my face.

"Have you been tempted?" he asked.

I fumbled through a series of "ums" and "wells," stuttering until I gave up and smiled.

"It's okay," the bishop said. "We're all tempted. Moral character is defined by how we react to temptation. I hope you'll continue to consider your moral character in the face of temptation. And Jenny's, too."

I assured him I would, and we both stood, shaking hands. I excused myself and wandered through the empty church halls, treading on the brown carpet past the chapel, stocked with plain wooden pews. I couldn't imagine then that the room would be the venue for one of my most dramatic and regrettable performances.

Wednesday

I know Jane can't leave me. She knows I'm irreplaceable, and I'm glad because frankly I don't want to replace her. We have got a good thing and not everyone can keep a perfect balance like we do.

"Are you coming with me or not?" Jane demands.

"Why does it matter where you live?" I ask. "I don't want to live in California."

"Well, I do," she says.

"Why can't we just keep doing what we're doing here?"

"I'm tired of being here."

Then I say: "Look, I want you to stay."

Jane starts to melt and I feel a little guilty for employing such tactics, but the truth is I *do* want her to stay. But I also know it's only because I want to sustain what we have and that someday our relationship will inevitably ebb and float away.

"I can't imagine staying here." Her voice softens.

"What you imagine happening somewhere else is exactly what will happen here," I say.

"What does that mean?"

"It means that if you're going to run, make sure you're running *to*, and not *away*."

"I'm not running *away* from anything," she shoots back.

"What are you running *to*, then?" I ask.

"I'm not running, *period*." Her voice grows louder. "I'm simply just *tired* of here." The emphasis on "tired" insinuates that she is tired of me, too, but I pretend that I'm oblivious and I just sit there and smirk.

"Why do you have to be so confrontational all the time?" I ask, knowing what this will do to her.

"Me? You're the one that's confrontational."

"And defensive, too. You're always defensive about something." I am pouring gas over the fire.

"You are probably the most impossibly"—she angrily spits the words out at me—"most fucking impossibly . . . *stupid* fuck—"

"Stupid? Is that the best you can do?"

Jane lunges for me, at first in anger, but soon we are both on the floor of my living room, laughing so hard we have to hold ourselves.

"You really are stupid," Jane says, still laughing. "You know that, right?"

"Yeah, I know. So are you." I kiss Jane on the forehead. We lie there silent for a minute, and then I tell her, "I hope you stay." It comes out sounding like an apology, and in a lot of ways, it is.

Journal #2

When I was first shipped to Phoenix, we took a car trip to a cabin my first cousin twice removed owned up on the northern rim of the Grand Canyon. As we ascended out of the valley, I remember worshipping the beautiful red rock formations and the cacti and the vast sky that opened up in front of me. But I also remember feeling afraid. I stared at a cactus in the distance and thought, *I could get hurt out there.* I stared at an endless brown field, every acre a carbon copy of the rest, and thought, *Everything here is dead.*

We stopped in Sedona for lunch. I went into the gift store of the restaurant to look around while my first cousin twice removed finished eating.

"Don't dawdle," my guardian warned. I was careful not to linger looking at any one thing for too long. I wanted a magazine for the ride back. The gift shop didn't seem to have any. I really wasn't surprised when I returned to our table and my guardian was gone.

Without panicking, I walked out to the parking lot to confirm that I'd been left behind. I headed back toward Phoenix on foot, looking over my shoulder now and then to see if any of the approaching cars were being driven by my first cousin twice removed. None were.

Less than a mile out of Sedona a white pickup truck pulled over.

"Where you going?" the guy—a rancher—asked, vaguely concerned.

"Phoenix."

"This is your lucky day," he told me.

I hopped in the truck, which smelled of dust and sweat and dogs, and we raced down the highway. The rancher asked me typical hitchhiker questions, and I made up a story about how I was seeing America via my thumb. The rancher liked this story, as much as he didn't believe it, and launched into one of his own about how the youth of America weren't as patriotic as they were in his day and how more people should get a feel for the land, to cultivate an appreciation for what nourishes and sustains them, and I nodded my head all the way back to Phoenix, thinking, *Christ, what a bummer.*

Essay #4: Amends

Dr. Hatch wanted me to call all the people I'd hurt and ask them for forgiveness. It was part of the program, Hatch said, like the essays and the journal and the writing exercises. Child molesters called their sons and daughters, adulterous husbands called their wives and said sorry. Didn't I want to call Karine? I couldn't make Hatch understand: I didn't hurt anyone.

Here's what happened: I met Karine one night at La Onda, the bar where I worked in Boca Raton, my attempt to put Jenny behind me for good. Karine hung around the bar most of that night, talking to me while I poured drinks. At first I thought she was merely friendly, or lonely. As the night wore on, I could tell that Karine was hanging around waiting for me.

"My shift's about over," I said to her. "You want to get out of here?"

"What do you have in mind?" she asked.

I cleaned empty glasses and wiped the bar in front of her.

"Nothing in particular," I answered. I told Karine she could come upstairs to the apartment that came with the job and wait while I changed. She said sure, she could do that.

After showering, I came out into the front room and Karine was sitting on my couch, looking around.

"I hate to wait," was all Karine said, but it was the way she said it that let me know she didn't actually want to go anywhere, that what Karine really wanted was for me to give her one good time in the vacuum of the dreariness of her life.

A surge of power came over me and I sat next to Karine on the couch. She seemed even sadder when I got up close to her, but instead of feeling sorry for her, I reached out and stroked her arm. She flinched but didn't make a move to resist, so I leaned over and kissed her hard on the lips. I could taste alcohol on her tongue, but I didn't gag, and she put her hand on the back of my neck and forced her vodka-soaked tongue all the way into my mouth.

We sat like that for a while, until I moved to untuck her shirt. Karine helped me by wriggling a little and I lifted it off over her head. Soon we were both naked and on the floor. I crawled on top and started kissing her madly, really getting into it, until she pushed me away.

"Do you want to stop?" I asked.

She just looked at me.

"We'll stop if you want to," I told her, but she didn't say a word and I put my hand back down between her legs and she started moaning again.

Just when we started to get back to where we were, I could feel Karine hesitate once more. As much as I wanted to give her what she needed, I couldn't spend a lifetime doing it, so I quickly moved inside her. Her whole body tensed up. I was gentle. She tried to fight it, but I felt she wanted me to take control, to convince her of what she wanted. When we were through, she was in a hurry to leave and I didn't get a chance to hold her. I guessed she didn't need that part of it.

We Finish Nice Guys

The first thing Dale wants to know is what it's like in rehab.

"Is it like in the movies?"

"Worse."

Dale and I are waiting for the bartender to notice us at the crowded bar. The restaurant side is pretty empty, and we could easily get a table and have our drinks delivered, but the thought of being chained to a table for an entire meal with Dale is too intimidating, especially without Talie as point man for topics of discussion and interesting interjections.

Dale is satisfied with my answer and doesn't need to hear any details, which surprises me. Talie's letters to me at SRC were full of details about this "great guy" she met through a friend of hers, and since most of the guys I knew at that time weren't "great" in *any* sense of the word, I secretly began to look up to Dale, or at least the ongoing composite of him drawn from Talie's letters.

It surprised me how much something so little could mean. Somehow it pleased me to know Dale drove a blue Volvo, that Dale had his clothes dry-cleaned, that Dale took Talie out faithfully every Saturday night. Dale is in real estate in a way that's too complicated for me or Talie or anyone we know to really understand. I imagine

Dale in dark oak rooms with dim light, convincing people to buy, or sell, or to buy more, to lend him their lives.

I didn't expect Dale to be a pretty boy when I finally did meet him, when the two of them picked me up from SRC. Obviously, Talie had told Dale about me; he seemed "ready" to meet me. I could tell he was putting the nice on a little when he shook my hand. That would have been okay—I almost expected it—but I recognized Dale right away as one of those ironic guys, dangerous because they could draw you out with sympathy and mock interest, and then leave you flapping your arms uselessly in the air.

"What are the tricks to getting attention?" Dale asks.

"Wave money," I suggest.

Dale pup-tents a twenty and waves it at the bartender, who registers us with a side glance.

"Look at that," Dale says as we sit. He nods at a guy approaching two women at the bar. We watch like kids in front of a TV, waiting for the shuttle to lift off, anticipating the noise and smoke and breaking apart of intentions, of ideas. "God, I'm glad I don't have to work for it anymore," Dale says.

"Yeah," I agree, trying to figure out if that means Dale's glad he found Talie, or if it means something more sinister.

"I could never really get into it," Dale goes on, still staring. "I mean, I always felt like women knew what I was doing when I was on the make. How could they not?"

This question pretty much says it all.

"Did you say you have to go back?" I ask. It seems like a lame thing to ask, but I'm having real difficulty coming up with things to say.

"Uh, yeah," Dale says, sips his beer. We're both confused about this, him not remembering if he told me he had to go back to work or not, me not sure either, whatever.

There's a pause, followed by a critical comment of someone's appearance, followed by another drink, followed by a pause, and so on.

"Where did you say you had to go earlier?" I ask, remembering something he said on the phone.

"Oh," he says tiredly. "I had to meet this old cocksucker friend of mine from school at Propheteers. He's an investment banker from New York and was meeting a client there for dinner."

I quit lobbing questions altogether as Dale leans back in his chair, liquefying.

"I'm really in love with Talie," Dale says, nodding grandly, his head tomahawking through the fog of cigarette smoke.

"Yeah?"

Dale, swear to God, puts on his puppy dog face right there at the bar. "I can't believe I found someone like her," he says.

I'm thinking, *Please, Christ, don't start crying.*

"Well," I say.

"You've got to convince her to marry me," Dale says, reaching out and grabbing my arm. His vise grip causes an involuntary recoil and he lets go.

"Yeah, sure," I say. I look away from Dale and into the gaze of two women at the bar checking us out.

"You see those hooks looking at us?" Dale asks without moving.

"Yeah," I say. "I see them."

"I shouldn't call them hookers," Dale says, apologetic. "They're not as dignified as whores."

I notice: *Hey! Dale is drunk!*

"See, hookers were great." Dale leans in. "They knew what you wanted and you knew that they knew."

I wonder if Talie knows about this. "Didn't you worry about diseases?" I ask.

"I did get something, once," he says. "I gave it to my bitch girlfriend, too."

I was hoping I wasn't ever going to hear the man who was thinking about marrying Talie use that word.

"I mean, I didn't have *that* many," he says, guessing what I was thinking. "It just worked out."

He sits up and smirks, satisfied.

The women are no longer looking at us.

"I know a lot of women who aren't vultures," I say, making what I think is my point.

"Some women aren't," he agrees. "And not all men are assholes, either."

"True," I say.

"I mean, look at us: We're nice guys. We're the exception."

Here Dale realizes he's talking like a drunk and shakes himself, draining the alcohol from his mind.

"They're looking again," Dale says.

I smile, a little amused, both by the women and by Dale's delusion that he is a nice guy. The more I think about it, the funnier it gets.

Journal #3

That's me at the conference table with two FBI agents, the seat still warm from Teddy, who had finished his interview a few moments earlier, his last question to the agents, "Should I get a lawyer?" jangling my nerves.

The summer after my emancipation proved a watershed time. I'd enrolled in summer classes at Glendale Community College to gain a head start on those who had the advantages I never would, a plan that evaporated the moment I encountered Talie having lunch in the atrium of Scottsdale Fashion Square with an older man. My immediate thought was that Talie had found her birth grandfather, but Talie had never mentioned any sort of search for her birth family. Instead, Talie introduced her lunch companion as Jay Stanton Buckley, founder of Buckley Cosmetics.

I'd heard of Jay Stanton Buckley before his name became a regular fixture in the papers, though. Randolph College Prep boasted a Buckley Hall, the honor bestowed after Buckley donated a nice sum toward the construction of Randolph's library. JSB also regularly placed in the top ten of the Phoenix 40, an annual compilation of the forty wealthiest and most influential businessmen (whose sons invariably attended Randolph). Certain titillating rumors about JSB reached the populace via profiles in newspapers and local magazines: that he hopped between real estate holdings by helicopter; that he kept a private plane in a hangar at Sky Harbor International; that he hired only young, staggeringly beautiful secretaries, who were collectively known as Buckley's Angels.

I had all of this in mind when I arrived at Buckley Cosmetics for the interview Talie had arranged when I mentioned that I would never be truly emancipated without my own money.

Buckley's offices on Camelback Road consisted of two buildings—a two-story building that housed administration (top floor) and legal (bottom floor), and a single-story building that housed accounting. An impressively clean driveway separated the buildings, the asphalt tributary running around back to the employee parking lot, each space carefully stenciled with the initials of the space's owner. At the far end of the parking lot, a basketball hoop mingled with the fronds from a neighboring palm tree, which was undergoing pruning by the team of Tongan landscapers imported from the archipelago of South Pacific islands by JSB himself, all outfitted in turquoise polo shirts bearing the Buckley logo.

The receptionist invited me to wait in a nearby conference room, showing me to a couch in a room towering with boxes. Through the floor-to-ceiling drapes I could see men in suits sauntering through the hallways. The electronic buzz of the switchboard was nearly constant.

The conference room door clicked opened and a man in his early seventies appeared, closing the door behind him. "Hello," he said, introducing himself as Dr. Theodore F. Weber. "You can call me Teddy." Teddy asked me a few questions about myself, genuinely interested in the answers. Eager to talk about the job, I mentioned that Mr. Buckley had made a generous donation to my high school. "That's the kind of man he is," Teddy said enthusiastically. "If you come to work for us, you'll see that for yourself. The thing is this: We all work for Mr. Buckley. He's the captain of the team, and everything belongs to him: the bats, the balls, the playing field, everything. And we're his team." That was the closest we'd get to discussing the job. Instead, we diverged into the fact that Teddy had come to work for Mr. Buckley through his son-in-law, who worked at Buckley, after running a successful medical practice in Chicago. He'd moved with his wife to Scottsdale to be closer to his daughter and had magically been tapped by Mr. Buckley to head up the department of runners, the foot soldiers that were the backbone of Buckley Cosmetics.

"So when can you start?" Teddy asked.

I told him I could begin immediately.

We stood and shook hands, and like that I was Buckley Cosmetics' newest runner, a position I learned had an amorphous set of responsibilities. There were certain absolutes: The three supply rooms, one on each floor of both buildings, were to be inventoried and restocked daily; the out-of-state lawyers fighting JSB's various legal wars were to be shuttled to the airport on Friday afternoons and picked up again on Monday mornings; a catered lunch was to be provided daily on each floor, each entrée from a different restaurant (JSB's theory about this was that if he catered lunch, the lawyers were less likely to disappear for hours in the afternoon); the buildings were to be opened at 7 a.m. and closed at 7 p.m. I came to understand that the largest responsibility, by far, was to be ready to be called into action should the need arise: a last-minute run to FedEx; spinning one of the family's Mercedes through the local car wash; beating the clock at the courthouse clerk's office with a legal filing, etc.

My first day on the job, I was certain I'd made a serious error in judgment.

"We could lose our jobs any day," my fellow runner Trish said on my inaugural courthouse run. "We're all just waiting to get fired. A lot of people have already quit."

Trish's grim prediction spooked me. I'd hoped that I'd quickly rise through the ranks to more hours and more money. More importantly, to be identified with Buckley, a brand everyone knew, would go a long way toward obliterating my anonymous past. The possibility that the opposite would happen was a disaster, and I began to wonder what I'd do if it came to pass.

I envisioned myself a foot soldier under JSB's command.

And no job was too small.

When JSB needed someone to fetch a tie from his gleaming mansion, I volunteered, punching in the gate code, letting myself into the empty house. My worn loafers clicked against the Italian marble floor as I took in the spectacular view of Phoenix from the kitchen bay windows. I opened the refrigerator to peek at the groceries of the rich and famous, expecting the labels to be fancier, the foods richer, surprised by the inventory of everyday brands you could find in *anyone's* refrigerator. I traipsed through the tastefully decorated living room (furnished with the same style and color of furniture as the Buckley offices) into the master bedroom, a room as large as the front room. I stood before the bathroom mirror and ran my fingers through my hair, marveling at my infiltration of such a nice house. I thought about how my ghostly footprints would never be known by JSB or any of the fabulous people who most certainly came through JSB's front door, how once I stepped back out into the driveway, it would be like I'd never been here.

I finally saw Jay Stanton Buckley again the second time I paid a visit to his house, some two months after I started working at Buckley. JSB sometimes liked to walk the few miles between the office and home for exercise (shrugging off the concerns for his safety from the investors who wanted his blood, according to the papers), and so one of the runners would drive his Mercedes to his house at lunch, with a runner in a company vehicle following. As the last hire, I was never offered the lead position in this two-car caravan; but one day JSB walked home without notifying anyone, calling for his car after all of the other runners had gone home, save me and Trish. Trish had no interest in driving JSB's Mercedes (she was afraid she'd wreck it), and so I confidently took the keys from Teddy, barely hearing his warning to be careful.

I had, to that moment, driven every car in the Buckley fleet except JSB's Mercedes. Once every week or so, two runners would spend an entire day driving the company cars through the car wash that was a mile or so away, including the company's twin tan Cadillac limousines, which sat like sleeping tigers in the back of the employee parking lot. But I'd never been closer to JSB's Mercedes than walking by it on my way into the building (it was the lead position in the row of employee parking, closest to the door, and directly in sight of JSB's office window, so I rarely stopped to admire it). It was like no Mercedes I'd ever seen, and there was a rumor that it had been imported from Europe. The dark blue interior matched the custom paint job, and I had to adjust the driver's seat to account for the difference between JSB's 6'2" frame and my 5'11" reach. I carefully started the immaculate car, the dashboard and stereo lighting up as I surveyed the gauges and JSB's preset radio stations. After adjusting the rearview mirror (but not the side mirrors; I couldn't figure out how), I backed the car out of its spot and pulled into traffic, Trish behind me in the company van.

The drive up Camelback Road to JSB's house was a short one, but I savored every mile, the Mercedes floating along the streets, banking softly with the slightest turn of the steering wheel, as if the machine were reading my mind. I eased the car into JSB's driveway, punched in the gate code, and touched the accelerator to climb the sharp incline. My instructions were to leave the keys in the car, but I recognized my chance and strolled through the marble portico and knocked on the solid wood of the front door. Trish threw her hands in the air and shrugged, and I smiled back.

The heavy door swung open and JSB stood towering over me, beaming, his jacket and tie replaced with a polo shirt bearing the Buckley logo.

"I . . . I brought your car," I said, stammering, caught without anything to say.

"Great!" JSB said. "Do you want something to drink?" He stepped back to let me in.

"Who is it?" a voice asked. A smallish, impeccably groomed woman appeared from the kitchen. "Oh, hello."

"This is Charlie," JSB said. "He's a good guy." JSB slapped me on the back with a force that propelled me forward. That JSB knew my name was an unaccountable thrill.

"Very nice to meet you," the woman said.

"Here are the keys," I said dumbly.

The woman disappeared into the kitchen and JSB followed her, reappearing with two cans of soda. "For the road," he said. I took the cans, wanting instead to be invited for dinner, to eat from expensive china and hear conversations littered with references to JSB's friends: Ivan Boesky, the Wall Streeter who was eventually busted for insider trading; Michael Milken, the genius junk bond financier at Drexel Burnham whom the government charged with securities violations (my economics teacher at Randolph, a former broker at Drexel, first introduced me to the idea of junk bonds, and to the name Michael Milken; he began every class by pulling a bottle of Pepto-Bismol from his leather briefcase and chugging a healthy swig); or Sir James Goldsmith, the billionaire merchant banker.

I relished the idea of annotating this fantasy dinner conversation with what little I knew about anything, indicating gently that I was willing to learn, wanted to be an apprentice.

My new ranking among the runners was quickly apparent when Teddy approached me about a mission JSB wanted carried out. The noose was tightening around Buckley Cosmetics, it seemed, and JSB was making plans for life post-Buckley, having rented office space up the road for a real estate consulting firm. Few knew that JSB had handpicked a group of executives to move with him to this new business, and he wanted to furnish the new offices with furniture from the Buckley offices. So as not to alarm those employees who were not in the know, the furniture would be moved before and after working hours, JSB and others placing a small orange sticker on items that were to be moved up to the new offices.

Secrecy was an essential element of the transition, and Teddy deputized me and Lance, another runner, for this very important responsibility. At first, Lance and I moved effortlessly, making a run in the morning and one in the afternoon; the offices up the road filled quickly with expensive furniture. We moved silent as cat burglars until a marble credenza we could barely lift wouldn't fit in the elevator.

"Should we even be doing this?" Lance asked me, exasperated. Lance had, from the outset, agreed to the mission simply because he wanted the overtime.

"I'm sure it's fine," I replied, unsure if it was or not.

"Then why do we have to sneak around like this?"

I smelled revolt and did my best to quell it. "Teddy wouldn't involve us in anything underhanded," I said, a truth Lance couldn't deny.

Lance waited with the credenza, which we parked in the atrium of the small office building, the other occupants glancing at it curiously as they filed in for another day at the office, while I called

Teddy to apprise him of the situation. The twenty or so tenants seemed to know that Jay Stanton Buckley was moving into their building, and they watched from their windowed offices as Lance and I brought expensive piece after expensive piece through the front door, up the elevator, and down the hall to the newly rented corner offices.

Teddy's instructions about the credenza did not make Lance happy.

"This is ridiculous," Lance said as I relayed Teddy's directive to take the credenza to the unused stables on JSB's property.

The code for the back gate was the same as the code for the front, and we committed the combination to memory as we punched it in time and time again, the gates opening slowly as we ferried the overflow of furniture to the stables. Three or four runs in, Lance asked to be relieved of his overtime duties, and Teddy took his place without comment, gabbing with the Tongans who landscaped JSB's property while we unloaded our take in the crisp fall morning air. I hoped JSB would remember my stamina when he made the move from Buckley to his new offices.

My interest was more than simple employment: If I could catch JSB on his next upswing, a new life could be made, I guessed.

The government had caught wind of JSB's intention to flee, and upon my early arrival one morning I was met with the unhappy news that the FBI wanted to talk to me and Lance and Teddy. In fact, Teddy was already being interviewed in the conference room in legal. I sprinted across the compound to find out what was going on, a wild look in my eyes, bumping into William, a Southern lawyer who worked for JSB.

"What is it?" he asked.

I explained to him what was happening and he called me into his office and shut the door.

"What's the truth about the furniture?" he asked, sitting behind his desk.

I told him the whole story, about Buckley's new offices, about the moving expeditions before and after work, about the stash of furniture in JSB's stables. A horrified look clouded William's face. In the short time that I'd known him, I'd come to know that he was an aboveboard guy who did not tolerate dishonesty.

"My advice is to tell them the whole thing," he said. "It's a felony to remove property from a bankruptcy estate." It was the first time I understood that Buckley Cosmetics had filed for bankruptcy, rather than having the impression that it was an option. William's words were not the legal comfort I was searching for. I wanted him to jump out from behind his desk, outraged, ready to defend me against the crush of a maniacal government run amok.

It occurred to me that I might be in real trouble and I cursed JSB for putting me in a vulnerable position.

The conference room door swung open and a red-faced Teddy charged out, asking over his shoulder, "Should I get a lawyer?" The two young, fresh-faced FBI agents answered that that was up to him. Teddy spotted me coming out of William's office. "The boys had nothing to do with it," Teddy added.

"Thank you for your time," one of the agents said, motioning for me to take a seat at the conference table.

The legal conference room was a naturally dark room, its eastern exposure partially blocked by the accounting building across the compound. The FBI agents did not turn on the lights, but took their seats across the table from me. The credenza populated with tiny crystal tombstones commemorating Buckley's various product launches caught what light was available, twinkling like a constellation behind them.

"We already know from Teddy about your recent activities," the one agent said. "We just want to hear it from you."

The agent's use of Teddy's nickname frightened me.

"Are you aware that what you've done is a crime?" the other agent said. "One felony count for each item removed."

I looked the agents in the eye. I wanted to let them know that their tactics didn't scare me, but it wouldn't have been the truth. I told them what they wanted to know. Teddy had failed to mention the cache of furniture on JSB's property, and I drew them a detailed map, providing them with the gate code, the last ounce of loyalty draining from my body.

I'm Good for One More

A ringing phone in the middle of the night is always bad news, but when Talie's out with her friend Holly, it's always the same bad news. "Charlie," Talie's voice falters on the other end. "Will you pick me up?"

I try to rationalize, try to say it might be something else, too drunk to drive, lost her keys, *anything*.

I wish Talie would've called Dale, but Dale wants to marry Talie and something like this might change his mind, even though Talie has never said she wants to marry Dale.

I'd like to see Dale handle this one.

The scene at Holly's is as predictable as it was in high school, and I get into my old routine: ask Holly how Talie is, how it happened, who this time, where she is now.

For a change, Holly isn't acting groggy, like she doesn't know the details.

"It was this asshole from Texas," she says, crying.

Cowboys. I can't stand them. Many cowboys have seen the inside of Holly's apartment, which looks newly cleaned, each magazine and remote control whisked back to its proper place in anticipation of after-hours company. It's not me she had in mind when she cleaned earlier.

"She didn't do anything," Holly is saying, defending Talie's behavior. I haven't even accused anybody and Holly is spinning the defense—this is how bad it really is.

There's common knowledge between us: I think Holly's a slut, so she can't help but not like me. The first time I was hauled out in the middle of the night, my sophomore year (there was a guy who had Talie's shirt off in the backseat of Holly's car), Holly didn't say anything to me. Instead she stayed in her room while Talie explained very rationally about the four maybe five tequila shots that had poured her into the backseat of Holly's car.

Now I'm listening to what Holly's saying, marking her words, "innocent," "charming," "seemed," "drunk," "outside." The last word I hear makes me wish I *were* outside, listening to the little sounds the night makes when everything is where it should be in the world.

Holly can't force the narrative together and she breaks up, crying to the point of heaving, but I know no matter how bad it is in here, behind that door, inside her bedroom, it's much, much worse.

Talie's on the bed in the dark and I go to her.

When I wrap myself around her, she smells of alcohol and says it feels like she's hurt for real. She doesn't say anything else, doesn't cry. I don't either.

"It's okay," I tell her.

She says my name with a weak voice.

"Yes?"

She's silent, whimpering a little, and I let up on my grip, gathering her around me, waiting for what's next.

It's the first time we involve the police.

I love that Talie isn't embarrassed by the questioning, the photography. Talie answers the questions as they're asked. I listen to the description of the perpetrator, hear his name, how it happened.

I hear the words "not my fault" and I wonder about them, keep hearing them over and over.

I'm asked some questions too. Being in the police station creeps me out.

The officer seems to suspect everything, what we've said, how his desk is arranged, the way the sun starts coming up outside his window, people he works with saying hello.

They want to talk to Holly too.

I give my answers, saying things like "I can't say" or "I don't remember."

I remember coming close to being here once before but don't tell the officer. A friend of Talie's, in from out of town, some guy she knew once from somewhere. He left town before I got a chance to confront him. Talie didn't spare me anything. The way she told it, he was all over her, but not at first. At first, always, everyone is innocent.

We are finally released into the early morning and I drive us home in silence. Talie leans her head against the cold window but doesn't close her eyes. I wish we were on our way to dinner, or to a movie, or to anywhere but Arrowhead.

Thankfully, JSB has left for the office before we get back.

"How can you sit there and take it?" Talie asks, standing in the kitchen.

I ask her what choice I have.

"You can stand up and do something," Talie says. "Are you going to let this happen to me again?"

"I'm not letting anything happen," I tell her. I want to get out of the kitchen and into the living room, but Talie has me trapped. "Why didn't Holly try and stop it?" I ask.

"She did try," Talie says, yells. "She climbed on his fucking back, but he knocked her out." She starts to cry but won't let me comfort her.

"I don't want you to hang out with Holly anymore," I say, half saying it, floating a test balloon.

"What?" she asks.

I don't let her scare me off my point.

"Everything bad happens when you're with Holly," I point out. "I just would rather you didn't—"

"She's my friend," Talie says. "She tried to *help* me."

"I don't believe you," I say, a statement that confuses her, and she backs down.

"I can't believe you won't do something about this," she says. The phone rings and it's Holly, my argument over. Talie recounts our early-morning activity and I'm forgotten in the kitchen. I'm planning my escape when I hear Talie in the other room, "Oh, really?" loud enough to know that it somehow involves me.

"Well, *someone's* going to do *something*," she tells me, hanging up the phone.

"Who? Holly? She's done enough."

Talie shakes her head. "Dale."

"What's he going to do?" I ask.

Talie just shrugs. "He's going to do what any *man* would do," she says.

"Not a *rational* man," I say, getting mine in too.

"Whatever," she says, her key to many victories in our past. The phone rings again but I don't wait to hear who it is, imagining it's Dale, calling to detail his plan of action.

The bar at the County Line is two deep all the way around, and I have to wait a half an hour for a small table in the corner. Several at the bar fit the description Talie gave the police, any or all of them looking capable. The one on the dance floor, some honky-tonk with a halo of sweat from his hatband, becomes the focus of my investigation. For a moment, I fear for the woman he is dancing with, but then he turns, faces me straight on, and his weak jawline and sloping nose exonerate him.

The two women behind the bar, older, late forties and all sex, are making the drinks so efficiently the drinking at the bar seems to increase, heated talk rising up toward the ceiling fans, where it's spun around and forgotten. Two cowboys at the table next to mine rise up suddenly and one's on the other, knocking over their chairs. I'm ready for the riot, the beer and the bad energy flowing through me, when the jukebox quits midway through a Hank Williams tune.

"God damn it," someone yells, a body moving through the crowd. The jukebox is plugged back in and then the brawlers are shown out. I'm ready to leave, satisfied with having made an effort, hoping it brings redemption in Talie's eyes, when I spot the suspect sitting at a table in the opposite corner, quiet and alone.

First off, he's smaller than I pictured. Talie's description made him out to be large and bulky, yet he's nicely wedged in the corner, out of sight. He doesn't seem to be looking around and doesn't look up when someone backs into an empty chair at his table. Someone else asks if they can take it, and he lets them.

I forget what he's done for a moment and understand why he did it. In this place, Talie and Holly very easily would have been the most attractive—if not the only—women around. If I were this guy, and those two let me buy them a drink, let me dance close with them, twirling in the cake-clumped sawdust, I wouldn't have expected them to say no, and I probably wouldn't have believed them when they did.

Keeping an eye on his table, I call the police, who tell me to stay where I am, which is what I plan to do. I'm going to wait ten minutes, giving the police some travel time, and then approach him, maybe push him around some. The other option is to charge at him with a broken bottle, a move I've never made, unsure if I'd be able to actually stab someone, something I'm pretty sure you'd have to be sure about before breaking the end off of a beer bottle.

I'm admiring the different-shaped bottles at the bar, sizing each up for grip, and when I look back at the table in the corner, Dale is leaning into the guy. No one seems to notice, none of the backs at the bar swivel around with interest. Dale hoists the guy out of his seat and drags him toward me.

I'm not happy to see either one of them.

"Charlie, meet Shane," he says. Shane is struggling in Dale's grip and doesn't look at me. It strikes me that Dale isn't surprised to see me.

Shane is dragged to the parking lot, more by Dale than by me, but I get a hand on him too. What exactly Dale has in mind isn't known by me, but whatever it is, it's going to take place in the darkened end of the blue-and-yellow-neoned pavement. Shane is forced to hug a telephone pole while Dale ropes his hands together.

"Do you know this guy?" Dale yells at Shane, pointing at me. Shane sees me for the first time and doesn't recognize me. "Do you?"

"No," Shane says. "Fuck no, I don't."

"You raped his sister," Dale reminds him.

"I didn't rape her," Shane says, which sends Dale off, a few kicks landing in Shane's stomach, landing him on the ground.

I'm bothered that Dale refers to Talie as my sister, which she obviously isn't, instead of as my girlfriend, and it's definitely something to ask him about later, but I'm too impressed by his heroics, and the old feeling of admiration I had for him from Talie's letters returns.

"Charlie, get what's on my seat," Dale says.

I walk slowly to Dale's truck, hoping the police will show up before this goes into real violence. I pick up the baseball bat on Dale's front seat. The aluminum is cold and round and I heft it over my shoulder. I hit a piece of asphalt from the parking lot into the trees. The bat lets out a *ping* when I connect, and the sound travels to distances beyond where we're standing.

Shane cries out as I slam the door. A few guys stumble out of the County Line but make so much noise they don't hear anything.

Shane's in bad shape now, his pants thrown up on the car next to us, a beer bottle wedged mouth-first up his ass. The thought occurs to me that whoever was drinking from that bottle earlier had no idea how it would be repurposed.

"It won't be as bad if you say you're sorry," Dale is telling Shane.

I don't think Shane buys it. I don't.

"Man, I'm telling you, I didn't rape her," Shane says, crying, I think.

Dale whips the bat out of my hand, swinging it again and again in the air, warming up. A car pulls up behind us, the headlights shining so that I can see a few swallows of beer left in Shane's glass tail.

Holly and Talie get out and Talie gasps when she sees Shane.

"Dale, don't," Holly says. "Don't do it."

"Why not?" he asks.

"Tell them what happened," Shane pleads, then angrily, "Tell this psychopath what happened."

Before Holly can say anything, Dale brings the bat straight across. I kick the bottle away a moment before Dale connects, but he doesn't seem to notice or care. Shane screams, the only one not afraid to speak. Holly and Talie are silent; Dale just grunts as he hammers away. Shane's shrieks get softer and softer and less insistent as he slumps and slides to the ground.

"I'm going to be good from now on," Talie promises, whispering it in my ear. She reaches for my hand, locking her fingers into mine. Her grip on me tightens. She smiles as the yellow and blue neon gives way to flashing red and blue and we all scramble into vehicles, not turning our headlights on until we're blocks away from the County Line.

Journal #4

My relationship with Jenny began to feel like a separate life, one with a separate set of friends and venues (church dances, cards and board games at her house, or the occasional date now that she was sixteen). The serenity the relationship bred when I was with Jenny convinced me that we belonged together. But the fact that I hardly talked about her when I was with Talie, who still didn't know much about her, or with my friends, who knew her about as well and saw her even less, or with anyone at Buckley Cosmetics—Jenny's mother thought JSB a crook and forbade me to mention his name—drove a wedge in that serenity and I began to be aware of a split personality I had inadvertently developed: the caring and loving husband type I exhibited when I spent time with Jenny, and the adventurous nighthawk that combed the streets late at night with my friends, looking for something interesting to do, like the rave at the Icehouse, an abandoned meatpacking plant in downtown Phoenix, hosted by a former porn star who was embarking on a new career as a DJ. As Jason and I twirled with the crowd of drugged-out teenagers, I wondered what Jenny would say if she could see me.

Or if she could've seen me at the warehouse party Jason and I crashed after a fruitless night of asking adults in 7-Eleven parking lots to buy us beer. The warehouse was in a notoriously bad part of town. A homeless shelter was nearby and even the police seemed to ignore the war zone. The only parking spot I could find for my beloved Pulsar NX, purchased with the help of the Chandlers, who had all but adopted me, was on a dark street around the corner, and so midway through the keg party in the unlit, windowless warehouse I stepped out to move my car closer to the front of the building, skipping quickly through the deserted streets. Upon my return, I noticed a large man standing in the center of the floor without his pants. As my eyes dilated, readjusting to the darkness, I noticed that the woman standing next to him was naked too, and that other guests were in the throes of removing their clothing.

"Time to go," Jason said, grabbing me as we launched out into the night.

I tortured myself over what to do about Jenny. I knew I loved her, and I loved how we complemented each other. I couldn't imagine anyone with finer qualities and I knew it would be a waste and a shame if we didn't end up getting married. Marriage to Jenny was my only road to salvation and redemption, I knew. But the universe was unattuned and just saw us as kids. I allowed myself to indulge in self-pity about having met the perfect mate too soon, the self-pity inducing the feeling that I was the victim of cruel fate. A breakup seemed inevitable, an idea that reduced me to tears when I considered it. I had no idea how to undertake something as emotionally devastating as ending a great relationship without cause. I knew it would come out of the blue, shocking Jenny and our mutual friends, dynamiting a cornerstone of my otherwise fly-by-night life. The best I could do was write Jenny a letter, cowardly sending it to her through the mail, asking her not to contact me for a month but to meet me thirty days later in the courtyard of the Biltmore Fashion Park, an upscale outdoor shopping center where Jenny and

I sometimes had lunch. I hoped the month off would prove to Jenny that she could get on with her life without me, a wish I wanted for myself, too.

I lay awake the night before our reunion. I felt silly for having asked her for a month's worth of silence, and a little surprised and afraid that she'd assented, without so much as a hang-up phone call over those long four weeks. I didn't know any more than I knew a month earlier, and I wondered if Jenny had solved anything. The answer to the latter was quickly apparent as she strode up to me in the deserted Biltmore Fashion Park courtyard, letter in hand, launching into her response to my letter, the bitterness of the response having grown exponentially while it festered for thirty days.

I sat there listening, knowing I deserved every word of it.

The highest emotion one human being can have for another. There is no greater feeling than showing affection and having that affection reciprocated. It's possible to feel different degrees of affection, depending on the nature of one's relationship to another person. Without a doubt, the most gratifying form of affection exists in a realm of physical and sexual freedom. A realm without judgments.

Most people live in a world of constraint, where affection is merely reciprocated, like a game. I do something nice for you, you do something nice for me. While this existence is placating, there is no real emotion, only prescribed emotion.

Free from constraints, however, a person is allowed to indulge in the kind of affection a relationship can create. A person is allowed to give as much affection as he wants; and more importantly, he is allowed to take as much affection as he needs. Each is totally satisfied.

Take Karine, for instance. A good example. Karine had existed for so long on the crumbs of affection various men in her life had thrown at her that when Karine happened into La Onda that night, she looked like she hadn't eaten in days. Even though I didn't know her, I put myself at her mercy. I pretended that I had the utmost affection for her (I'm sure I would've developed a sense of affection for her, given time) and gave her all the affection I possibly could, replenishing her. It was just that she was so shocked that she didn't know how to react, she wasn't used to the wonderful feeling of unbridled affection. She just couldn't . . .

Maybe Karine's a bad example.

I arrive to find Jane on the couch, naked, watching TV. I sense she is about to be coy, but then I notice (sigh) Jane has been crying. I sit down next to her, blocking the view, and she pulls her feet up so that her heels are in her crotch.

"What's the matter?" I ask.

"Nothing." She looks over my shoulder at the TV.

"Tell me what's wrong." I rub her knees tenderly. "What is it?"

"Nothing." She sniffs quietly, dramatically.

"Something must be wrong, Jane," I sigh.

"I can't decide what to do," she blurts out.

"About what?" I'm massaging her thigh now.

"About anything." She starts to cry.

"Like what?" I'm beginning to be agitated.

"I just can't decide about . . . California or here . . . or you or . . ." Her voice trails off.

"What do you think you should do?" I ask, genuinely trying to help.

"It's just that I know [*sniff*] that I'll [*sniff*] meet someone like you in California and [*sniff*]—"

"What does *that* mean?" I pull away from her.

"That my life [*sniff*] will be the same . . . wherever I go."

"That's probably true," I say coldly.

"I'm fucked up." She really starts to sob, but it's just a ploy because she knows she has upset me, and I go for it, putting my arms around her.

"It's okay." I try to calm her. "You're not fucked up. You're going to be fine."

"You really think so?" she asks, pressing a wet cheek against my neck.

"Sure." I pat the back of her head and right then I hate her more than I've hated anyone in a long time. The way she smells makes me crazy and I jump up off the couch.

She looks up. "What's wrong?"

"Nothing."

"No, really, Charlie." She stands up, fully naked in front of me.

"I just wish you'd make up your mind about us." I try not to look at her.

"I know. I'm sorry," Jane says. "I just don't know what I want."

"Well, you better decide."

I make myself cry, and this moves Jane to put her arms around me. I struggle out of her grip and stand there with my head down. When I look up at her, fake tears sliding down my face, she's looking away, at the TV.

Essay #6: My First Time

I like hair. All kinds: brown, black, red, blond, long, short, curly, wavy, straight—whatever. And skin. I can't get the feel of skin out of my dreams.

When other guys were showing their prowess at basketball on the playground at recess, Steven Howfield and I were starting clubs and trying to get girls to join: Saturday Afternoon Club (weekly picnics designed to be romantic, like on TV); Very Secret Society (initiation included kissing both Steven and me on the lips for ten seconds—we promised not to tell anyone, hence the name); Daisy-Chain Gang (the main function of this club was to play out a bizarre game Steven and I had concocted, the rules of which I have forgotten); and the Millionaires' Club (we tried to convince cute girls that we were going to be lawyers and that we'd make a lot of money). Once Erica Ryan and I stayed out on the playground after the bell, hiding in the corner where the gymnasium joined the administration building, and we kissed until Ms. Fisher, our fifth-grade teacher, realized we were missing and came looking for us. Erica and I had to stay after school with our heads down on our desks until her parents and my grandparents came for us. I peeked over my hairless arm several times, but Erica would not look back at me.

And at Erica Ryan's birthday party I was the only boy (Steven Howfield was particularly pissed at being snubbed, but losing out to guys who are better than you is something you can never learn too early in life) and my grandmother was hesitant about letting me go. Imagine what it was like to be the only boy at Erica Ryan's eleventh birthday party. Imagine being locked in a closet full of gloriously dirty laundry and Erica opening the door after counting to sixty and yelling "Here!" Imagine Erica Ryan throwing her older sister's bra at you. Imagine her slamming the door shut again and all the girls giggling. I had never smelled anything more wonderful than that bra. Imagine me pressing the cool fabric against my forehead. Imagine me inhaling.

Years later, in San Diego, I babysat for my divorced piano teacher, Ms. Thomas, who gave lessons out of her house. I was her favorite student. She would sit next to the bench and point along to the music with her slender fingers as I tried to keep up. She smoked a lot, but once you were in her house for a while, you hardly noticed it.

One night I babysat her two kids, Harry, eight, and Sidney, six. I put them to bed at nine, like Ms. Thomas had told me, and I knew she wouldn't be home before midnight, so I had plenty of time to myself. I normally don't like to snoop around because I am impatient and don't know what to look for, but something was clearly drawing me to Ms. Thomas's bedroom.

The dark was cool, and after my eyes adjusted, I could make out a dresser, a bed. The room was a mess, clothes thrown everywhere. I stood motionless, breathing in the peculiar scents the room held.

I moved over to the dresser, opening the top drawer and pulling out one of Ms. Thomas's lace bras. The silk and lace sent an electric charge through me, and without even thinking about it, I unzipped my pants and put the left cup over my erection, letting it hang like a lace flag in a stifled wind.

I'm not sure what made me commit the act. I'm not even sure where the idea came from, except that suddenly I was on my knees at the foot of her bed, and the bra with my cock wrapped inside it was wedged between the mattress and the box spring and I began moving back and forth, like I'd seen in cable movies. It felt awkward at first, a little rough even, but then it smoothed out and felt all right and I was really moving. A couple of times it slipped out and I had to readjust the setup. Right when it started to feel the best, I began to sweat. I moved a little faster and then something went wrong. I wanted to scream. I stopped moving but something was happening and it felt like someone was cutting me with a knife. Finally it stopped and I pulled everything out and felt the hot goo puddled in the left cup. I buried the bra in the rest of the dirty clothes and got out of the room as quietly as I could, shaken and exhilarated.

For a Good Time Just Call

Jane and I have a game that we sometimes play where I leave and come back.

I cruise around the block while Jane tucks herself into bed, and when I come back, I pull a ski mask over my face and crawl through the front window of her apartment. The place is dark and I feel my way around the living room to the bedroom. The door badly needs to be oiled, but Jane pretends she doesn't hear it squeak.

I leave the door open and pounce on the bed, startling her awake. I press my hand over her mouth and her eyes get wide, a suitably terrified expression comes across her face, and I growl: "I've seen you . . . I've been watching you." On some nights Jane works up tears, and the wetness on my fingers really makes me violent. "I'm gonna make you really cry and *you'll love it*." Jane nods fearfully.

"I'll bet you've got a pretty pussy," I say, and pull the sheets back. She clamps her knees together and folds them up to her chest, but I slip one hand between them, breaking them apart while unzipping my pants. "Show me your pretty pussy," I say. "Here, pretty, pretty, pretty."

I pin her arms to her chest and put all my weight on top of her so Jane can't flail around. I kick out of my pants and boxers. "Shush now," I say to quiet her sobbing, and I pretend that if she's quiet, I'll pull my hand back. At this point she begins to whimper and this is usually when I enter her. "Oh, yeeeeees," I moan. "You have a pret-ty pus-sy, pret-ty pus-sy," I sing as I hump to the rhythm my words are making.

After I come, I pull out and roll off her. Jane gasps for air. We both grab for each other's hand. We lie still for a moment, not saying anything, and then Jane mounts me until she comes too.

Journal #5

The week Tim was suspended for starting fires in the boys' bathroom, my reputation was revealed to me. Principal Edwards had summoned us for interrogation simultaneously, and everyone was shocked to see me return to my seat so soon. I imagined the others regarded me with an air of caution, wondering what I would do to retaliate against those who had nominated me to the principal's ears. I dreamed of radical terrorism, toilets spouting like fountains, poison ivy on the swing set, ink in the lunch milk, the entire playground on fire. Transferring schools seemed bad enough, but transferring from Rapid City to San Diego in the middle of my freshman year was socially disastrous. Not picked for basketball or football or baseball, Tim was the only other kid no one wanted anything to do with. "Those guys are a bunch of fags, anyway," Tim said. "Humping each other over a little ball. Fuck 'em."

Tim and I spent most of the time hanging out after school at Tim's hideout, a tin construction shack left by the crew who had paved the highway behind my new home. We called it the clubhouse. It could hold up to five people, but only Tim and I ever went there. Weeds sprouted up inside the shack, nourished by the shaft of sunlight the doorless entrance allowed. We collected cans there, rummaged from the Holiday Inn Dumpster down the highway, and cashed them in at the local recycling center. Weekends were our big score. In addition to the cluster of beer cans, we usually came away with a full library of porno magazines discarded by weekend surfers. When the bell rang at the end of the school day, Tim and I raced to the clubhouse and spent the afternoon leafing through the fleshy pages.

Tim learned the delivery schedule at the Texaco next to the Holiday Inn and knew that when a truckload of goods came in, one of the clerks would have to leave a register to check them in. The other clerk was usually overwhelmed with cars pulling in off the freeway.

So we started stealing beer.

First it was six-packs behind our back. Then we started walking out with a twelve-pack each. Olympia. Hamm's. Pabst Blue Ribbon. I selected mine more on the basis of color and design, but Tim always stole Coors.

"My dad drinks Coors," he told me. Tim's father left his mother when Tim was five. Tim never talked about him, except he always told me that his father drank Coors. I wondered if it was the only thing Tim knew about him. A small picture on the hutch in Tim's apartment showed the three of them. Tim was in his mother's thin arms. His father had his arm around his mother. They both had long, thin faces with eyes the size of marbles, and their hair was identically feathered in the style of the times. I never told Tim that my parents died in a gas explosion before I could really know anything about them, back when I lived in Sacramento. That was before I was shipped from relative to relative, first Denver and then Santa Fe and then Rapid City.

We added our empties to the aluminum heaps outside the shack.

"Look at this," I said, fishing a used rubber out of an Old Milwaukee can. The tip was full and it was tied off in the middle.

"Gross," Tim said, coming closer. He knocked it out of my hand and stepped on it. The white fluid leaked into the dirt. "Have you ever used one?" he asked.

I shook my head.

"I have," he said. "On my neighbor."

I looked at him skeptically.

"Really. You can too, if you want. She's about forty," he said. "She's a mental defect, though. She sits on the curb and drools on herself all day."

We really did find Dora on the curb, just like Tim said. I'd seen her before but thought she was just waiting for a friend, or the bus.

"Hi, Dora," Tim said.

"Hi, Tim," Dora said without looking at him.

"This is my friend."

"Hi," Dora said without looking at me. She seemed to be concentrating on something in the distance.

"You want to go inside?" Tim said.

"No," she answered. She shaded her thick-framed glasses and turned her head up to get a look.

"C'mon," Tim said. He pulled Dora by the arm and Dora rose like a genie.

"Let go," she said.

"C'mon, Dora," Tim said, gently turning her toward his apartment. "Let's go inside."

"I don't want to," she said. "I'll call the police."

I grabbed Tim's arm. "Man, don't." I tried not to sound panicked.

"Don't worry," he whispered. "She isn't going to call the cops."

"I am," Dora said. "I called them last time."

"Yeah? And what did they tell you?" Tim asked, smiling.

"They told me not to let you do it again," she said.

"Did the cops really come?" I asked worriedly.

"Yeah, they came. Didn't they, Dora? You called the cops on Timmy, didn't you?"

"Yep, yep," Dora said.

Tim grinned and I looked away, Dora's gaze following mine, trying to see what I was looking at.

Dora began waiting for me on the curb in front of her apartment, three doors down from Tim's. Her last name was Wells. "I think I'm English," she said. Dora would say things like that that would crack me up, without trying to be funny.

What Dora told me about herself wouldn't be more than an hour's conversation no matter what day of the week it was, but she parceled the information out over time. She was born in San Diego and had never left. Dora didn't have any other friends besides me, she'd lived in her apartment for more than twenty years (before I was even born, I thought), and her parents lived "somewhere else." Someone from a special service came and checked on Dora twice a week, bringing her a small amount of marijuana to relieve the shooting pain in her eyes. The only thing Dora loved was bingo, so three nights out of four we'd take the bus to Our Lady of Hope, smoking a plump joint on the way.

Even though the bingo hall was the size of a double-car garage, they somehow managed to pack in more than two dozen people every night. The room was charged with nervous excitement. Dora played faithfully every week but couldn't seem to win. And it didn't appear to bother her. She only ever talked to one other person besides me, one-armed Eva. Eva's husband axed off her left arm in a blind rage. "He was cuckoo," Eva said, laughing like the joke was somehow on her. I liked Eva's sense of humor. She could really work her bingo marker too.

Dora never played for more than a couple of hours. I'd sit in the corner, propped up on the stool with the wobbly third leg, smiling for good luck when Dora turned around in her metal folding chair. I didn't mind waiting; bingo didn't interest me. I liked to sit and picture myself on the stool, like an image from a satellite, and wonder if any of my old friends back in Rapid City would recognize me. I wanted to see the look on Lloyd Inman's face when he saw me with Dora. Man, old Lloyd would've been surprised. The whole gang would've. Zeke and Bruce and Georgie and J.P.

"Okay," Dora would say when she was finished. We'd hold hands while we waited for the return bus. Once or twice Eva took us out for a late dinner at Hardee's or Arctic Circle—the only two places where Eva would eat. But it was usually just me and Dora. We'd spark up down the street from Our Lady of Hope and imagine we could hear the 57 bus before it turned the corner. The bus driver would accelerate on the freeway on-ramp, Dora's face pressed against the window, the yellow freeway lights flashing by like lightning.

I didn't tell Dora about the note someone passed me the morning after Tim's suspension. "I never knew you were a fag," it said. Someone had written "Me neither" in blue, curlicued letters. I turned around in my desk, but everyone was staring at the chalkboard, intently watching Mrs. Riggins explain algebra. Heat flashed across my forehead and I stood up and walked over to the trash can. Mrs. Riggins stopped the chalk and everyone was looking at me. I crumpled the note into a ball and dropped it into the garbage. Mrs. Riggins waited for me to reach my seat before she continued.

"What do you and Tim do up in the shack by the highway?" Tony Richards asked me at lunch. Now that I was infamous, I'd tried sitting at the popular table.

"Suck each other's dicks, probably," John Killspotted said.

Everyone at the table laughed and looked at me. I tried to laugh with them, to take the joke, and Greg Knot pointed and said, "Look, he likes it too."

Tony's sister, Lucy, spit out her mashed potatoes, laughing.

I picked up my tray, my hands and arms shaking.

"Oops. Time to suck a dick," someone said, and the table erupted.

The others started in too. John Killspotted said he'd heard I was in the hospital and asked if it was to get my stomach pumped. Greg Knot told a disgusting story about a gerbil.

I set my tray back down on the table. "Listen, fuckers," I said. Nobody moved. "Tim's the fag, not me. In fact, when he gets back, I'm going to kick the shit out of him." I was shaking as I said it, and when Tim came back a week later, I was even more nervous. The whole school was talking about it and I was worried Tim had heard what I'd said. John Killspotted put his finger in my chest at lunch and said, "We're coming up to your love nest. We expect you're going to do something about Tim."

"Yeah, okay," I said. I felt Tim's eyes on me. John Killspotted walked away and I set my tray of turkey and gravy down across from Tim.

"Why are you talking to that Injun?" Tim asked.

"He asked me if I would do his homework," I lied. "And I told him, 'Fuck no.'"

"Doesn't surprise me," Tim said. "Stupid fuckin' Injun."

It was for reasons like this that I hadn't told Tim about Dora. I had been grounded by my aunt and uncle when report cards came out, and I told him I was still grounded to keep him from calling me up. I always ran to the door at Dora's in case Tim was looking out the window.

"Hey, do you want to meet at the clubhouse after school?" I asked nervously. "You know, drink some beers."

Tim looked across the table and smiled. "You mean you aren't going to visit Dora?" he asked.

Hearing her name in the cafeteria caused me to blush, and I stammered, trying to deny it.

"It's cool," Tim laughed. "I won't tell anyone." He shoveled a forkful of corn into his mouth. "I mean, that pussy's pretty sweet," he said. He smiled as he chewed. "And *easy*."

A sick feeling came over me.

"She can't keep her mouth shut about you," Tim said. He winked. "I think she really likes you."

"Yeah?" I asked weakly.

John Killspotted walked by the table. "After school, then," he said, and walked away.

"What's after school?" Tim asked.

"That's what I meant to tell you," I said. "When I told that fuckin' Injun that I wouldn't help him, he called me and you fags, so I told him to show up at the clubhouse after school. We'll fuckin' show him who's a fag."

Tim put his fork down. "Fuck yeah. I hate that Injun anyway."

"Meet me up there, then," I said, and picked up my tray. I spent the rest of the afternoon in the nurse's office with a sick stomach, sprawled out on a cot, staring at the ceiling.

John Killspotted and Greg Knot met up with me as I climbed the hill toward the shack.

"Hey, fairy," Greg Knot said.

John Killspotted laughed. "Hey, Tinker Bell."

"Shut the fuck up," I said, walking in front of them, as if I was eager to get to where I was going.

"You better beat your boyfriend into the ground," John Killspotted called from behind. "I'm not coming up here to watch you two make out."

We passed a group of sixth graders who had just gotten off the bus. "There he is," one of them called out, and the pack fell in behind me. I saw myself from the satellite again. I saw Zeke and J.P. and the others looking too. This would remind them of Dallas Tucker, the new kid at the high school adjacent to Knollwood Heights whom everyone had heard about, the beating and the disappearance. It occurred to me that I, too, was a member of that phantom class. I never even knew what Dallas Tucker looked like. It galled me to think everyone back in Rapid City would probably remember us both in the same breath.

I thought about the satellite picture and heard what anyone who knew me before would've thought out loud: *Is that really him? Is that where he went? It doesn't even look like the guy we knew. It must be a mistake.*

I didn't see Tim at first, but he poked his head out when he heard the excited voices converging. He glanced at me and then at the crowd behind me, confused. He started to say, "What the—," but I rushed up and shoved him to the ground.

"Shut up, faggot," I said. Tim tried to get up but John Killspotted kicked him hard in the stomach. Tim doubled over and the others started chanting, "Get him, get him." John Killspotted nodded, menacing, and I hauled off and kicked Tim in the crotch, my foot aching. My blood surged, rushing through me, my skin pinpricked. Images of Zeke and Bruce and Georgie and J.P. swirled across my field of vision and I buried my foot again and again into Tim, who curled up on the ground. He wore a quizzical look and I thought of Dora and I kicked him again, tripping and falling over his shaking body. Greg stepped up and kicked Tim and kept kicking and the crowd kept chanting and finally Tim rolled over onto his stomach and quit moving. John Killspotted said, "There you go, faggot," and kicked Tim hard again and Tim groaned.

I pushed through the crowd and ran. I could hear Tim's groans all the way back to my house.

After bingo, Dora asked if I wanted to stay awhile, but I said I should probably go. Tim's window was dark. The temperature had dropped suddenly and the wind cut through my jean jacket. I hugged myself as I waited for Dora to put her key in the lock. All the apartments resembled one another from the outside, each unrecognizable from the next. Once Dora was inside, I kissed her good night. She waved to me from the window, but I was distracted by the large chunk of siding still missing from the corner apartment building. Tim and I had blown it away with a shotgun Tim's uncle had left behind. I guess I was surprised no one had fixed it. I felt the jagged groove. Tim was gone. I felt it right then. The next morning I would hear about how someone had called an ambulance, about Tim pissing blood. By lunch it would be confirmed that Tim's mother had transferred him to another school. Dora wouldn't know anything about Tim and Tim's mother moving out, a young couple with an infant moving into their old apartment. Dora wouldn't have any idea about her having to move apartments either. Less than a month later, I would be standing in front of Dora's, peering through the ghostly curtains at an empty apartment.

The houses across the street were strung with lighted candy canes and Santas, but the apartment buildings remained dark. The holiday season had begun across the street and on the street over and block after block throughout the city. I can't remember what I got for Christmas that year. By then I had moved again, to Phoenix, where there aren't any seasons.

I Take Jane on a Hot-Air Balloon Ride

Here's the key to any relationship: surprise.

Surprise breaks the repetition that is the death knell of all contemporary unions. That's why for Jane's birthday I surprise her with a sunrise hot-air balloon ride/champagne brunch.

There is nothing more magnificent than watching the sun rising over the desert (except maybe watching the sun *setting* over the desert). Jane loves it. We stand holding hands and look out at the eastern horizon, spellbound. Looking down, we watch the shadow over the desert floor slowly pull back, revealing its harsh landscape, awakening wildlife.

Our pilot pours us champagne and we eat fresh fruit with our fingers, ignoring the handsome pastry display.

"Happy birthday." I kiss Jane on the cheek.

"Thank you." Jane smiles.

We hardly speak the rest of the ride. I can tell she is totally enraptured and this makes me feel good. It's a good feeling to treat people the way they deserve to be treated, according to Dr. Hatch, and he's right.

In need of money, I took a part-time job at Pete's Fish & Chips. Over the first few weeks, the regular set of customers slowly became known to me. One customer in particular, a comely woman in her late twenties with a young daughter, ate at Pete's with a frequency that shamed the other regulars. I soon learned that the woman and her daughter lived in one of the three low-income houses that shared Pete's asphalt parking lot, housing that was clearly from another era and was one development phase away from being leveled. The woman's daughter liked to ride the mechanical pony under the awning out front, and I began slipping the girl quarters as I chatted with her mother while they waited for their order. We talked about my situation with Jenny, me couching the demise of the relationship more in terms of my not being Mormon, which I'd come to blame as the truth.

"That's a tough one," she said. She told me how her husband had deserted her and her daughter, an idea I obsessed over between her visits. I wondered what kind of person could do such a thing, disappear on purpose.

A loneliness descended upon me as Christmas neared, and an innocuous conversation with the woman about the holiday deepened the feeling.

"Buy your tree yet?" I asked as she hung around the front window.

She shook her head no. "It's either buy the tree, or buy something to put under the tree," she said. The answered floored me; having a Christmas tree ranked up there with the other inalienable rights Americans enjoyed. Determined to right this enormous wrong, I borrowed my friend's truck and bought one of the last Christmas trees available from a corner stand, stopping at Target to purchase a bag full of bulbs, lights, and tinsel. I enlisted the help of a coworker to help me drag the tree to the woman's front door, the coworker happy to be excused from work. The woman answered my knock, perplexed.

"Merry Christmas," I said, smiling.

She arched her eyebrows. "You playing Santa?" she asked. An awkwardness descended as my coworker and I stood supporting the wilting tree.

"Thought you might like to have a tree for that present," I said.

The woman smiled awkwardly and stepped aside, admitting us into her tiny living room. That the tree was too big for the living room didn't diminish my enthusiasm, and my coworker and I quickly strung the lights and hung the bulbs. The woman's daughter peered around the corner, scared at the sight of the monstrous tree.

"It's a Christmas tree," I said, plugging in the lights. The room was aglow in red and green.

"Want to see our Christmas tree?" the girl asked. "I made it."

"Sure," I said, caught up in the holiday spirit.

The woman folded her arms and leaned against the wall as her daughter led me around behind the tree I'd brought to show me a tiny tree she'd fashioned out of empty toilet paper rolls. The girl and her mother had glued cotton snow onto the tree, sprinkling glitter over the whole creation to give it the appearance of having lights. I stood grinning at the tiny tree, embarrassed as the girl excitedly ran through the various steps involved in making your own Christmas tree.

Friday

Cunt, cunt, cunt, cunt, cunt, cunt, cunt. Bitch cunt. It's fucking hilarious how women always say, "I want you to tell me what you're thinking about," and then they pull out of your life without so much as a "Had a good time!" or "Thanks for the cock!" Jesus, why?

I call in sick to Aztecka and then call back in ten minutes and tell them I'm quitting. Later I'm dressed up, leaning against the bar, and Jason is so pissed off at me he pretends not to hear my drink order. I wave down Miles and he brings me a vodka but doesn't take my money, and this gesture of kindness renders me mute.

It isn't long before I spot another one, alone at the table in the corner, but there is a revulsion within me, remnants of my loyalties to Jane, a revulsion I've felt many times before, the final pull of the last one's personality and the arrival of the next. The vodka clears the slate and I saunter through the crowd to her table and I can tell that she wants me to give her one good time in the vacuum of her life, and when I smile, she invites me to sit down and I do.

Essay #7: The End of Utopia

The end of Utopia comes in a poorly lit room, a wooden chair at the foot of a hospital bed. Outside the window a city carries on, ceaselessly. At the end of Utopia, I am sitting in a wooden chair, smoking a cigarette for the first time in my life, desperate for pleasure. My skin is a chemise that has been left out in the sun for too long. I want to get up and look out the window and see what's happening on the street below, but I don't have any strength. At the end of Utopia, I look over at a telephone on the nightstand next to the hospital bed and my mind is blank. At the end of Utopia, all I can wonder is what I had for dinner the night before. I draw on the cigarette and gag and it occurs to me that if I die, it could be days before anyone notices.

Jason's in his office at Aztecka after the place has closed for the night.

"Bitch," Jason says when I tell him about Jane. "What a bitch."

He looks up at me and says, "You're not gonna fuckin' believe this, but Sara's gone too."

I'm shocked by this but can't feel anything resembling an emotion beyond despair. "What a bitch," I say.

Jason looks back at his receipts, entering some numbers into the computer, the green glow of the screen painting his angry face.

Journal #7

My decision to join the Mormon Church was borne not out of religious zeal but out of romantic sacrifice. I wanted to prove to Jenny that taking me back hadn't been a mistake, that I could commit to our future. The anxiety induced by our separation drove me into a depression, the idea that I'd thrown away something of value plaguing my daily thoughts.

I kept my plan to be baptized Mormon a secret at first; Jenny was wary when I asked to start attending church with her and her family, sensing my motive. "You don't have to," she said, though I knew she was thrilled about having me in the pews on Sunday.

As far as I could discern, the Mormon religion seemed as harmless as any of the others, with the added advantage of securing the ribbon around my relationship with Jenny, whom I began to think of as my wife. We complemented each other nicely, and I noticed that the other Mormon couples did too, the women hanging on the men's every word, gazing upwardly at them lovingly, laughing at their jokes.

The first step to becoming Mormon was an interview with the bishop. While I knew the interview was a formality and that the bishop couldn't thwart my intentions, I considered the audition seriously; my preemptive loathing for the bishop as a potential obstacle powered an authentic performance that persuaded him away from his speculation that I was simply joining for Jenny, and I convinced him that my intentions were true and well considered.

The next step was a consultation with the missionaries. The elders like to convene with you in your home, but because I knew my first cousin twice removed wouldn't want Mormons in his living room, I arranged to meet them at Jenny's cousin's house. The missionaries took the regular-guy tack with me right away, a shtick they no doubt devised to play up their regional differences: one was from Alaska and one was from Texas. Elder Alaska was the quieter of the two, the foil to many of Elder Texas's jokes. Once we established that we were just three regular dudes, we proceeded with the business at hand.

"What do you know about the Church?" Elder Alaska asked.

I told them what little I'd gleaned from my limited exposure to the Church.

"We're ahead of the game," Elder Texas joked. "We normally spend the first interview correcting mistruths and rumors." A smile spread across his meaty face.

Elder Alaska produced a video and we settled onto the couch, Jenny's cousin and her cousin's family artfully dodging the front room as they moved silently through the house. The video dramatized the finding of the Book of Mormon, the lost addendum to the Bible, by Joseph Smith in upstate New York, the actor playing Smith effectively portraying piousness. Next the Mormon belief system was detailed: God as the Heavenly Father; Jesus Christ, his son; how Mormons can return to live with God through the atonement of Jesus Christ; the function of the Holy Ghost as a guide to help recognize truth; that the Church of Jesus Christ has been restored on Earth through the Latter-day Saints; how God reveals his wishes through modern prophets (as he did in his own time); and, most appealingly, that by leading an exemplary Mormon life of sacrifice and service, families can be together forever in eternity.

The elders asked if I had any questions and I shook my head, still absorbing everything I'd learned, connecting the dots between the ideas I'd heard uttered at dances and on Sundays and among the Mormons I'd known, the key to their secret language finally revealed. The question the elders were really asking was if I believed what I'd just seen—I imagined they were on the hook if they let a nonbeliever join for nefarious purposes, like wanting to marry another Mormon—but the question of belief didn't enter my mind. Sure, some of the LDS principles were hokey, but I weighed losing Jenny against having to pretend to believe in an afterlife and decided that the latter was nothing matched against the sorrow of the former. And so I accepted the pamphlets filled with supporting information and signed up for the conversion process, which consisted of a set number of meetings with the elders to prepare myself for baptism. Jenny's cousin was gracious to offer up her living room for these sessions so that I could continue my study in secret. By then, I was less concerned about my first cousin twice removed than I was about Talie finding out. For her part, Jenny continued to prod me with questions meant to ensure that I was acting of my own free will, my answers becoming more and more demonstrative as I pretended to embrace the Church.

The day of my baptism finally arrived. I'd chosen Jenny's father to perform the baptism, which involved full immersion into a tub of water. Arriving early Sunday morning, I sat in my car in the parking lot, the gravity of what I was about to do occurring to me for the first time. The absence of any family or close friends would not be a signal to the other members of the congregation, but I felt their absence and wondered if there was a tenable exit strategy. The fall from trying to convince Jenny that I was committed to our future to standing on the doorstep of conversion had been fast, and I looked around, a little shaken by what I'd done. Jenny's family arrived and I switched on the autopilot, smiling and shaking her father's hand. The parking lot soon filled with well-wishers and those brothers and sisters who made a sport of attending baptisms.

I waited in a small room attached to the baptism chamber, whose front opened out into the chapel. Jenny's father entered with our baptism suits, a one-piece long-underwear type garment that left little to the imagination. We both suited up and Jenny's father stepped into the knee-deep lukewarm water in the baptismal tub. He asked me if I was ready and I nodded that I was, wanting to be over and done with the embarrassing ceremony. The shield on the baptism chamber went up, revealing a gallery of smiling faces, ready to accept me into their fold. I looked away, not wanting them to be able to read my face or that I was preoccupied with how exactly my frame was going to fit into a tub the size of a small whirlpool. My concerns proved to be real when, during the ceremony, Jenny's father leaned me back for submersion and we both toppled into the water, his small arms unable to hold me as I fell backward. The crowd didn't react, and Jenny's father and I bounced up, drenched, the first part of the ceremony over.

The second stage of the baptism involved me ascending the pulpit to deliver my conversion speech, a talk I hadn't worked out in advance. I began by listing the litany of nice things I knew about Mormons, naming the Mormons I personally knew, breezing through Jenny's name so as not to give rise to speculation. I knew the crowd was anticipating my humbling, an act I understood from the missionaries (who were in attendance as the two required witnesses) was as much a part of the baptism process as the submersion. My eyes teared as a surprise homily about the importance of family and friends issued forth. The ghosts of everyone I'd ever known and would never know again floated through me as I completely broke down, sobbing, gasping phrases about how nice it was to be among so many caring people.

I Give a Handout

Some women don't know how well they've been treated. When Jane comes back, she's going to owe me a truckload of apology. If she tries to start up with another guy, she is going to see right away how superior utopian love is. Most men are only out to get. Take, take, take. Taking is a natural behavior, like for instance the guy with his sign, standing on the median across the intersection, clean shirt, blue jeans, worn tennis shoes. He walks along the median, pausing at the driver's side of each car for a three count before moving on to the next. The left-hand turn lane holds six cars at a time. The third car and fifth car give him money. The sixth car rolls up the window.

The sign says, FATHER OF 3, GOING TO BE EVICTED TOMORROW A.M. I see it when he swivels around and walks back toward his duffel bag, which is planted at the base of the traffic light. The car behind honks for me to make the right turn, and I almost go, but I see the girl in the seventh car, which is now the first, roll down her window.

The car honks again, and I switch on my hazards, letting traffic go around. The girl in the car is classically beautiful, the sort of vision of perfection you'd see on TV, and the guy with the sign doesn't move on after the girl shakes her head no. The guy goes into some kind of rap and the girl just stares straight, praying for the green light. I think I'm going to jump out of my car and maybe tackle this guy if I have to. The girl finally rolls her window up, pissing this guy off, and he smacks her window with his hand, yelling "Bitch!" just as the light changes and she speeds off.

I change lanes, drifting left, and flip a U to enter the left-hand turn lane.

"Spare any change?" the guys asks me.

"How much do you need?" I ask.

He says, "Whatever you can spare, man," without missing a beat.

"I can spare lots," I tell him.

He's never heard this and lowers his sign a little, looking me over. "A couple bucks would be good."

"I can give you more than that," I say. "Climb in, we'll drive to the ATM."

"I'll just take the change in your ashtray," he says.

"Look, the light is going to change and I'm going to drive away," I say. "Get in and we'll go to the bank and I'll give you a couple hundred bucks."

The light changes and he says, "Wait, man," and grabs his duffel bag.

The first thing I notice is that he doesn't smell like he's been standing outside all day. His hands are rough and he has the fingertips of a smoker.

"I'm Robert," he says, a little nervous.

I couldn't care less.

He starts his rap about how he lost his job (a lie, most likely) and then his wife left him (who would even consider marrying this guy?) and his children, oh, his children (they're better off).

"The world is a cruel place," I say in my best patronizing tone.

"You said it, man."

Robert stares at the mirrored bank building as if he is looking at heaven, turning in his seat when I pull around back.

Thankfully, there are no cars at the ATM.

"Wait right here," I say, and, just for sport, I leave the car running.

After moseying to the machine, I thumb through the cards in my wallet, standing out of range of the camera watching from behind the tinted glass. I look up and wave for Robert to come here.

He jumps out of the car, leaving the door open. "Yeah?"

"You're pathetic," I say.

"What?" He cups his hand to his ear, still walking toward me.

"Is two hundred enough?" I ask.

"Oh man, that'd be great," Robert says, putting his hands together like an altar boy.

"How about three hundred?"

"Oh, no." Robert shakes his head. "That'd be too much."

"Two hundred might not be enough, though."

"It's plenty."

"I think five hundred would be better," I say, nodding my head to make the decision final. "Yeah, five hundred."

We stand, looking at each other. "Man, you're jerkin' me around," Robert says, realizing something.

"No, really, it's right here," I say, opening my wallet. "Just take it."

Robert approaches me slowly, peering ahead as if afraid of stepping off a high cliff, his feet dragging loudly against the pavement.

"Just take my wallet," I say, folding it up and holding it out.

In the instant Robert reaches out, I grab his arm and whirl him around, slamming him into the side of my car. Too stunned to say anything, Robert tries to get his balance, but I kick him in the stomach and he quietly falls over.

"You shouldn't . . . *take . . . money . . . from . . . strangers.*" I get in his face. "You fuck."

Robert looks like he's sorry, that he'll never do it again, but this in no way satisfies me, and I prove myself to Jane and the world as a Great Defender by kicking wildly, and I keep kicking and kicking and just as Robert starts to scream, I hear a car pulling around to the side of the bank and I stand up straight, smoothing out the front of my shirt, feeling the sweat underneath, thinking, *Oh, God, Jesus, it's a cop*; but instead it's a white limo, idling. For a moment the whole earth is quiet. I can't jump in my car and drive away, since I'm blocked by the limo. Robert is writhing on the asphalt on the driver's side.

A chauffeur gets out and opens one of the limo's doors. A guy dressed in Bermuda shorts and a Duran Duran concert T-shirt steps out, looks over at us, looks away, steps up to the ATM. When Robert doesn't yell for help, I look down at him and see how badly I've fucked him up.

Another door opens and another guy gets out, dressed in a tailored suit—I can't tell if it's blue or black—and he looks so impressive I have to wave and smile.

"What's this?" he asks.

The guy at the ATM looks over at us.

I feel like this guy could really understand my anger, so I explain, pointing at Robert, "This guy was taking money by the freeway." I'm gasping, and the guy is trying to understand me. "He was slapping this girl around who wouldn't give him money."

"No, I didn't," Robert protests, crumpled in the fetal position.

"Yes, you fucking *did*," I yell. I'm so freaked out by the limo, the limo driver, the guy at the ATM, and the guy who is practically standing on my shoulders that I can't remember if that's exactly what happened, even though I'm pretty sure it is.

"Scumbag," the guy says, spitting on Robert.

"Let's go," the guy at the ATM calls out, and just as I'm about to say something polite like "Thanks for stopping by" or "Nice to meet you," the guy standing next to me kicks Robert in the head, once, twice, until Robert is unconscious.

All I can think is, *This guy isn't even sweating*, and his grin makes me step back.

The limo pulls away slowly, flowing through the outside teller channels. I jump in my car, maneuvering around Robert, trying to follow the limo, but the limo gets lost in traffic.

Best Man

Slowly I start toward JSB's office, the walls of the hallway lined with framed posters of past ad campaigns for Buckley Cosmetics, twenty years' worth. Sunlight wafts in from the rectangular windows above me. I stop in front of Talie's mother's layout, the one introducing her as the 1971 spokesmodel, her face peeking out from behind her long brown hair. She is dressed up like a mermaid, submerged in very blue water, her hair floating behind her, the words "World Gone Water" in black print floating around her. I'm staring into her eyes, wondering about the exact moment JSB decided that she was the most beautiful woman he'd ever seen. I begin to move away from the poster, watching Talie's mother's eyes as they follow me down the hall until I am out of sight.

"He left a message he wanted to see me," I tell JSB's secretary, and she nods that he's in and smiles. The double doors to the office are open and I feel the air become cooler as I step forward, the Oriental rug muffling my footsteps, the light from the picture windows causing me to squint. When my eyes adjust, I see the back of JSB's head, his hair trimmed tight. He is staring intently at the desert-landscaped inner courtyard, watching two speckled birds just outside the window. Boxes stacked in the corner lean pathetically and I feel myself begin to pity him. I stick my hand in my pocket and jingle my keys, warning him that I am coming up behind him.

"Hello, JSB," I say.

"How are you?" he finally says, swiveling around in his chair, looking me over, up and down.

"I'm fine," I say, not smiling.

A grin spreads across his face and he jumps to his feet. "I've got some news for you," he says. "I'm getting married."

"Really?" An automatic response. I get that familiar feeling that I'm misunderstanding something. "When?"

"Next month," he says. He's actually beaming.

"But I thought . . . ," I start. "The other day . . ."

"We're really in love," he assures me. "Will you stand in my line? Be my best man?"

"Of course," I say.

"And I want you to initiate a promotional contest for the new line of cosmetics," he says. "You can handle it. Just organize a party and make sure we get a winner. I'm going to fight this bankruptcy. I'm not giving up."

"Okay," I say, and it's a long time after I've left his office before I can even comprehend what any of this means.

Saving Room for Dessert

The dinner Talie has prepared is laid out on a small table in the corner of the formal dining room at Arrowhead. Penne pasta steams from a porcelain bowl; the single candle is reflected in the oval faces of the two china plates and silverware. "This is fabulous," I say.

"We're having a date," Talie says breezily, which explains her request that I wear a suit. She spins playfully, showing off her strapless black gown.

For the first time since Jane left, I sense that I won't go to bed with a gray feeling pulsating through me.

Talie tells me I look fabulous too and kisses me on the cheek. "A couple of us from the cotillion have been doing these mock dates," she tells me. "You know, to learn how to weed out bad men. I told you I joined the Phoenix Cotillion, right?"

I nod, vaguely recalling her telling me about joining what sounded like a girls' finishing school held on weekends at the Phoenix Cultural Center. "What's the sign of a bad man?" I ask, pouring a dark cabernet into her glass.

"There isn't one sign," she says. "It's an accumulation."

"What kinds of things do you talk about on these mock dates?" The pasta sears the roof of my mouth and I wince, flush it down with wine.

"The gentleman is supposed to lead the conversation. A lady punctuates with witty interludes and thoughtful asides," she says, quoting something. The echo created by the vast darkness of the dining room forces us to calibrate our words to low humming.

I tell her about Jane, lying that I don't really care that she's gone. I consider telling Talie about utopian love, about how Jane and I were a model couple, but her newfound stock in the conventional keeps me silent.

"Did you think you might marry her?" Talie asks, pointing up her beliefs.

I shake my head no. "Do you think you'll marry Dale?" I ask.

"No," she answers. "There's something bad about him. But he'll do until someone wonderful like you comes along."

"I'm not so wonderful," I say.

"You're a gentleman," Talie says, embarrassing me. "You're gentle and giving and, most importantly, considerate. Everything good stems from consideration," she points out.

"You're the only one who thinks so," I say.

"Actually, I did sort of meet someone like you," Talie says, giving up on her pasta. She pours us both another glass of wine.

"Really?" I ask.

Talie's secret lover's name is Frank, and Frank is a corporate attorney, which sounds like the cat's meow, and I get very excited for Talie, until I find out he's married, has two children, and lives in Scottsdale. Frank didn't call Talie like he was supposed to when his wife went out of town, which is why I was invited to dinner.

"You should see his little girl," Talie says. "She is so adorable."

"Are you sleeping with him here?" I ask.

"No, only when his wife is out of town," she says. "At his house."

We sit, not drinking, not eating, sharing our frustrations like we did when we were sophomores together at Leone Cooper High, before I transferred to Randolph.

"Is Frank a great guy?"

"Yeah." She nods, smiling. "Frank's a gentleman, too. He makes me feel at ease, you know?"

Talie's always given me great tips about how to treat a woman, and I log this one in. "Where does he take you?" I ask.

"Take me?" she repeats.

"You know, what do you do?"

"We generally just meet at his place," she says.

"Oh."

"Oh what?" she asks, anger in her voice.

"Nothing."

She closes her eyes. I surprise myself by reaching out and touching her face. Her skin is warm and smooth, and as I stroke the tiny invisible hairs on her cheek, she smiles. Her smile disappears and she opens her eyes. "I know Frank's just another user," she says.

"But you're in love with him," I say.

"I don't understand why he stays with his wife," she says absently. "I mean, can you?"

Wax spindles hang from the candle, which has been steadily melting between us.

"He's just having his cake," I tell her. "Forget this guy."

Talie looks away and I start to pull my hand away from her face, but she grabs my wrist, holding it steady while rubbing her cheek against my outstretched fingers. She stands suddenly, pressing her fingertips on the tablecloth for balance. I stand too, a reflex. She slips her arms under my jacket, clasping her hands at the small of my back, resting her head on my chest. She sighs dramatically, like Jane used to, and I embrace her, stroking her hair like I would Jane's when Jane was suffering.

"I should probably go," I say.

"I need you to stay," Talie says, pleading. She kisses me, tracing my lips with her warm tongue. I close my eyes, knowing if I stay, I'll be that much farther back on tomorrow, but Talie has always been stronger than me and I feel her hand inside my now unzipped pants. Talie reaches over and pinches out the candle with her fingers and she leads us out of the darkness, toward her bedroom, where tomorrow is farther away than the past.

Sylphs

Jon, a photographer for *Stylish* magazine who is in town to shoot the print ad for the new line of cosmetics, forgets to give me the password to get into Sylphs. Consequently, I get into a fight with the doorman, almost knocking him on his ass before Chandra Moses, one of the models hired for the campaign, arrives with another model I recognize from the head shots JSB approved, and I push my way inside behind them. I touch the photo of Talie inside my jacket that I want to show Jon.

We spot Jon at a table on the upper deck with two other models, Belinda and Alisha, and as we climb the wrought-iron stairs, I look down on the dance floor, watching the bodies swirling below me on the black concrete floor, the yellow lights cascading down on them. A free-fall sensation overtakes me as a woman passes behind me. The scent of her perfume is pungent enough to draw me away from the railing.

Introductions are made. The model with Chandra is named Kyle and has gorgeous black locks that bounce whenever she shakes her head. I have a difficult time not staring at all the cleavage that surrounds me, unlike the panting beasts who are circling our table three and four and five times to get a glimpse.

"I tried to get the whole balcony," Jon yells unnecessarily, and we wait for the end of this statement, but Jon just shrugs.

Alisha is listening to the conversation between Belinda and Kyle, of which I can make out only the names of perfumes, and I watch Alisha's eyes, childlike and empty as they drift out of the conversation and her gaze floats around the balcony, sizing everything up. I smile when Alisha glances over at me, trying to create some kind of conspiracy between us, unsure if Alisha even knows who I am, but she doesn't smile and simply looks away.

Chandra excuses herself and the men in her wake follow her exit.

"Did you hear about the place that does cosmetic cloning?" Belinda asks.

"That place outside the city?" Kyle asks.

"Yeah, at the Clinique de Hollywood," Belinda says. "They can make you look like someone else. All you have to do is bring in a picture . . . like getting a haircut, you know?"

"Is that legal?" I ask.

"It's just *plastic surgery*," Kyle says.

"The woman I saw on TV looks like Marilyn Monroe now," Belinda says.

"God, who would want *that*?" Alisha asks.

"Who would you be, then?" Belinda asks.

"I wouldn't even do it," Alisha says. "I think I look just fine."

"You do," Jon agrees. Belinda and Kyle look around, making eye contact with the men who are by now two deep. They flash winning smiles and Kyle even goes so far as to pout, giggling about it with Belinda. The guys nudge one another when Kyle looks away.

Jon puts his arm on the back of Alisha's chair and Alisha is visibly uncomfortable. I reach for the envelope in my pocket as a way to distract Jon, to stop his assault, but Alisha doesn't look to me for help, and I am confused as to whether or not she wants any.

I pull out the photo of Talie and slide it across the table to Jon. "What's this?" he asks.

"A local girl," I say. "I thought we might consider her."

"We've got enough models for the ad," Jon tells me. "Besides, I'm not allowed to use unagented girls."

Belinda and Alisha glance at the envelope, at me, and then back toward the crowding men.

"You should at least take a look," I say. Jon drinks his vodka tonic down to the ice and looks at me. "JSB wants you to consider her," I say. I know if I can get her this one thing, it might project her in another direction, away from Dale and Frank and even me.

Alisha catches the photo as it falls from Jon's indifferent grasp. "She looks nice."

"Her features are too far apart on her face," Belinda says. "Who is she?"

"I suppose your features are perfect," I snap.

"Well . . . ," Belinda says.

"Give it back," I say, reaching for the photo.

"Excuse me," a voice says. We all turn.

The guy Kyle pouted at stands in front of our table, trying not to lose his nerve.

"What?" Jon scowls.

The guy looks at Jon and then leans in over Kyle's shoulder, whispering something in her ear.

Kyle puts her hand on his cheek, turning his head, and whispers something back.

The guy smiles faintly and leaves.

Belinda laughs. "What did he want?"

"He wanted to dance," Kyle says.

"Why didn't you?" I ask, everyone turning to look at me.

Kyle glares at me and winces. "I don't want his hands all over me."

"Definitely a groper," Belinda says.

"This place is getting crowded," Jon says without looking around.

"Yeah, let's go," Belinda agrees.

"Where to?" Kyle asks, finishing her wine cooler.

"Caveat Emptor has a back room," Jon says, standing up.

"I'll meet you," I say, having no intention of letting this night drag on.

I toss the photo of Talie in the trash can in the men's room, knowing I could never look at it again without hearing Belinda's criticism. The bathroom attendant retrieves the photo as I push out of the bathroom, and I don't look back as I rush through a throng of people coming in the door.

Essay #8: Free Topic—Impropriety

It has only recently occurred to me that I open more doors than are opened for me.

I am keeping count.

Previously, I would hold doors instinctively, a natural reflex. And I believed that this was a form of common courtesy, that it was all about fellowship and kindness. But of course it has to be about much more.

I learned this as I listened to a woman, a peer, someone I don't really know, but someone I have held the door for, vehemently arguing that holding doors is an "undue exertion of influence by men over women." There were others who chimed in, talking in cool, clinical terms about things like "equality" and "empowerment." I could not fathom the implications of this conversation. Was common courtesy really an exertion of influence, a favor to be repaid, a debt? Does this mean that a smile or a look can suggest possibilities, make promises, imply?

There is a clear inequality between the sexes.

I have been privy to the secret conversations of men, the in-between comments, the raised eyebrows that telepathically communicate low whistles. There is nothing in these conversations or in this behavior that makes me think these things will ever change.

But I understand why things need to change.

I am on the side of progress.

To prove this to myself, I laughed out loud at a pair of city workers who slowed their truck as they passed a young woman striding along the sidewalk, yelling "Hey, baby" to her and bravely speeding up before she could respond. I laughed out loud at their pathetic existence. And as they passed me (I was just sitting at a bus stop, drinking a cherry Slurpee), the one in the passenger seat nodded to me as if we had an understanding. He thought I was smiling, approving of his behavior.

And I'm not sure I wasn't.

I mean, I saw the young woman first, before the truck came rolling down the street, before the catcall. I looked up and there she was in front of me. I did not say, "Hey, baby," either out loud or to myself, but I did make note of her appearance. That's all: I simply registered whether or not I liked how she was dressed.

But I know not to tell a woman that she looks nice, even though I am thinking that she does.

I've learned my lesson on this one.

I shouldn't even be thinking it, I know.

Because I know that by evaluating her appearance, I am objectifying her, making her an art piece in a museum of other women, and everyone knows that the objectification of women is the cornerstone of pornography and all this leads to the fact that I am considering her, rating her, telling her that I am willing to have sex with her. And I know that if a woman tells me that I look nice, that she likes my new haircut, that she likes the color of my eyes, she is really, subtly, telling me that she would like to sleep with me.

Of course Dr. Hatch disagrees.

I'm learning not to look directly at women I don't know. I understand that this is an invasion of their right to walk down the street unmolested. By looking at them, by trying to catch their attention with a smile or a look, I am frightening them, making them feel uncomfortable, demanding something in return.

Like a smile.

Or a hello.

Or a look.

I understand this completely.

I mean, I really do understand this. I understand that living among an enormously anonymous population can bring out the worst in people. It is very easy to hurt someone. Women have cause to be afraid. But most people are kind and treat people with the kindness and respect they deserve.

There are aberrations, of course.

The two girls we find in a club in Tempe—whose names neither of us can remember—promise they'll do a good job. Jason asks them several times if they've ever done a bachelor party and it's the blonde who says, "Of course not."

I am unamused by this blonde's cuteness, but Jason's panic at not reconfirming with the call girls we finally decided on after a night of endless interviews and evaluations is just now starting to subside. I give Jason the look I've been giving him all night, and he says, "I know, dude, I know."

The gathering of men in the suite at the Pointe South Mountain Resort hushes when the girls walk in. I think the blonde is named Tammy. The girls get back to back in the middle of the tightly mowed tan carpet. Ross MacDonald and Steve Speerman from the accounting department at Buckley jump out of the hot tub on the patio and come inside.

JSB is at the little bar in the corner with his back turned, but Peters from legal turns him around and they both fill their eyes with the two girls.

Everyone is waiting for someone to put the girls in motion, and I tell Jason, "Make them work."

Jason introduces the girls to everyone.

"This is Kiki and Cherry," Jason says.

"Hi, Kiki. Hi, Cherry," a unison chorus greets them.

The girls, whose real names aren't Kiki and Cherry, ask if there's any music, and Jason produces a boom box, which thumps to life. A couple lamps are switched off as the curtains sweep across the wall of windows looking out onto west Phoenix.

The couches and love seat are pushed back into a crooked circle, and any chair available fills the gaps until everyone is seated, JSB on the couch in the middle.

Kiki and Cherry dance the entire song without taking any of their clothes off. Their feeling that suggestive grinding and head rolling will put everyone in the mood fails to take into account that everyone was in the mood when they heard there would be a bachelor party.

Sensing the room's impatience, Jason yells, "Take it off, for chrissake."

Kiki and Cherry try to hide their panic as they lift their shirts off over their heads, buying them another thirty to sixty seconds of dancing before the crowd will want another sacrifice.

There's a knock at the door that no one hears but me. A fat man—two men, it seems—in matching Arizona State University sweatpants and sweatshirt shifts his weight in his maroon and gold flip-flops. The two call girls from the night before are behind him, leaning on the rail.

I step out into the hot night air and close the door.

"You didn't call, so we just came over," one of the girls says. She was the driver of the Lexus in the parking lot of the Circle K where we'd conducted our interview.

"You booked these girls," the man says. "I don't know what you've got going on in there now, but you'll have to pay for these girls." He nods in the girls' direction and his unshaven chin multiplies.

"Look," I say. "Somebody fucked up."

Everyone waits for further explanation, but I cross my arms and the four of us just stand there, waiting.

"We don't have to go in, but we have to get paid," the man says.

The master thespian would be good at this point and I tell everyone to stay where they are.

Inside, the music has stopped and Kiki and Cherry are on their knees naked in the middle of the circle, which has now collapsed in around them. Peters and MacDonald have their shirts off and JSB is on the couch in his boxers.

"Can I have my clothes back?" Kiki asks.

"We want to go," Cherry says, looking up at me.

"If you want to go, you can go," I say. A groan travels around the room. "The *real* girls are here," I tell the room, smirking at Jason.

A chorus of hurrahs chases Kiki and Cherry into the bedroom, their clothes thrown after them. The master thespian lets himself into the bedroom where they're changing, and I bring on the call girls, who you immediately know are going to give you your money's worth when they strip down and start fisting each other in the center of a newly formed circle.

"I'll let you know when we're finished," I tell the fat man, who stands post outside.

I look around to see if JSB is having a good time, wanting to see the satisfaction on his face, a look I single-handedly deserve for saving the fucking day here, but JSB has for the moment disappeared.

I check the bedroom and find Kiki and Cherry sobbing, half clothed, the trauma preventing them from getting fully dressed. The master thespian is sitting between them on the bed, and I'm about to say, "You're still going to get paid," when JSB comes out of the bathroom, still in his boxers, and walks past me without acknowledging me, then sits down on the other side of Kiki.

The master thespian looks up at me, smiles, and turns his attention back to Cherry, whose sobs are becoming less insistent. JSB puts his hand on Kiki's leg and she doesn't push it away. JSB says something in Kiki's ear and she laughs, two tears dripping from her chin onto his hand.

Cherry nuzzles Jason and he looks up at me and winks in a way that sends me to the moon.

"Never let another man take anything from you," JSB used to tell me.

"You have to reach out and take what you want," he'd say.

"Remember that you're the better man," he'd say.

"You'd be surprised who gets what they want," he'd say. "It isn't the one with the most talent or the most brains, but the one who perseveres. You have to be the last man standing," he'd say.

"Excuse me," I say, going into the bathroom, shutting the door.

I sit on the closed toilet and consider.

They were here first, it isn't that big of a deal, probably nothing's going to happen. You have to be the last man standing.

You're the better man.

None of them looks up when I open the bathroom door.

"Listen," I say.

Kiki and Cherry look up at me again.

"I'm sorry about tonight," I begin. "We really appreciate you making the effort you did—"

"It's okay, dude," the master thespian says, holding up his hand. "Everything's cool now."

MacDonald opens the door and I can clearly hear Peters's whooping. "JSB, you've got to see this," MacDonald says.

JSB, who I notice for the first time is drunk, slides off the bed, and MacDonald pulls him into the front room.

I close the door behind him and twist the lock. Kiki is staring blankly at the white light coming from the bathroom, and I slip in next to her. She may not even know what has just happened.

I overhear the master thespian say something about a shower and he and Cherry are gone just like that.

How to get from here to there: "Are you okay?" I ask.

It's the wrong thing to say.

"I'm fine," Kiki says.

"Wild night, right?" I ask.

She doesn't even look at me.

I can feel myself blowing it with Kiki. What I learned is that you have to just reach out and take something if you want it. Whether or not Kiki wants it is, for now, at this moment, a lost point. There is no indication that she *doesn't* want it.

There's a knock at the door and I hear JSB's voice.

"Charlie. Unlock the door."

The shower in the bathroom is running and I hear giggling.

Kiki looks at me, at the door, back at me, and I put my hand on her leg and decide what I'm going to do.

Journal #8

The last ice cube free-falls into the watery ice bucket. The ice machine rumbles angrily and then sighs, sputtering the last of anything it has, a spray of water coating the miniature glacier at the bottom of the bucket. I touch my wet fingertips to the corners of my dry eyes, blinking until the Aztec-patterned carpet comes into focus, my bare feet blending with the browns and greens, so that I'm convinced my toes are disappearing. I blink again and put one foot in front of the other.

Our limo driver, Happy something or other, rushes me when I push open the door. "Too stiff," he says, digging his tree-trunk fingers into the ice bucket, fishing for a chunk of ice. Behind Happy I see my new Jenny, her prom dress shucked in the corner in favor of her brother's army fatigue T-shirt and boxers, expertly holding a lit cigarette and a bottle of Budweiser in the same hand, waving from the balcony at someone as he passes underneath. The room's population seems to have doubled since my trip to the ice machine, other prom couples having found their way to the suite I rented for me and Jenny. I recognize the two foreign exchange students from Germany, Johann and Gustav, both with their hair dyed so blond they look albino; in the corner opposite the master race is Quentin, a second-year senior, and his date, Yesenia, who Jenny knows is secretly seeing either Johann or Gustav, I can't remember which. Jenny's friend Zach puts his arm around her on the balcony and they scream down at someone, Jenny losing her beer over the edge. The sound of the bottle crashing sends Jenny into hysterics.

Happy finds a piece of ice that will fit into his glass of vodka and tells me he'll be out in the car. He asks if I still need him, essentially asking if it would be better just to send the limo away, to stop the hemorrhage of cash, and I punch him in the face, my knuckles glancing off his flat nose, skimming his left cheek and ear. Happy drops the glass of vodka and, too stunned to say anything, runs out of the room holding his face.

Jenny pretends not to have seen, not wanting to acknowledge what I'm pretending to be capable of. She locks herself in the bathroom with Zach and the laughing continues, drowned out by the arrival of more prom couples, ones I don't recognize, who ask loudly where Jenny is. Someone turns on the television, which is sitting on the floor, as the credenza has been moved out onto the balcony for use as a makeshift bench from which to gawk at the other prom couples streaming into the hotel.

I'm just a kid. The echo in my ear since dinner, Jenny's justification for breaking up after prom, dulling the shine on the evening I'd spent weeks laying out. All gone with those four words. Where normally those words would've seemed a skip in a record to me, the turntable having been bumped many times before— sometimes my fault, sometimes not—I recognized right there under the white canopy of Octavio's that with the end of the evening, it would be over between us. My ego had conspired with Jenny to set me up for just such a fall: Jenny calling me her old man, whispering her thankfulness at being with someone who was "experienced," praising the maturity of our relationship, expressing her gratefulness at not having to stand around a keg in the desert, groped by novice hands, romanced by the indolent.

It was my idea, the whole thing, it always is, but I always fail to see—or rather, hope against hope that the entire house isn't built upon sand that can slip away with something like "I'm just a kid." My last Jenny had it sneak up on her, waking up one morning with the feeling that she was ready for what's next, not really knowing what next was. The Jenny before that accused me of keeping her eighteen, an accusation easily defended against by the lack of supporting evidence, of the nonexistence of her case, but even after the verdict was rendered in my favor, she left.

Someone in a tuxedo sticks his head in the door and yells that Vic is going to jump off the hotel roof, and while it seems impossible that everyone knows Vic, or cares about his welfare, the room empties, Jenny and Zach bursting out of the bathroom, the smell of marijuana trailing them out the door and down the hall. The TV blares in the sudden silence, a commercial for a compilation of hit music suitable for parties. Couples dance across the nineteen-inch screen, grooving to songs from my past, reminding me of all my Jennies. One song in particular feels overly familiar, and I mumble the lyrics along with the television, marveling that I know the words to a song I haven't heard in maybe fifteen years or more. The words come down from my brain as if I wrote the song, and I continue singing it even after the commercial has ended, am still singing it when a scream pulls me out the sliding glass door just in time to see Vic catch himself atop the building across the courtyard, windmilling to keep his balance. I spot Jenny and Zach, arm in arm, moving through the crowd below like celebrities at a charity event. The door swings open and Happy starts screaming in my direction. The officer puts my hands on the credenza and reads me my rights. The manager starts bitching at me about the state of the hotel room. Happy tries to get at me with a left hook, but the officer pushes him back. Vic teeters again on the hotel roof, the crowd below shouting up at him, Jenny shouting too, her pleas meant for Vic reaching my ears instead. I watch Vic trying to keep his balance. The officer wheels me around, and even though I couldn't pick Vic out of a lineup, I can feel him falling.

Ceremony

When Talie calls me from the cotillion, crying, I'm sure it's because of Dale.

So when I meet her at the Phoenix Country Club, I'm surprised when it isn't. Sure, Dale canceled out on Talie's cotillion at the last minute, but Talie is more upset that Frank wouldn't even consider it when she called him.

"What did you expect?" I say. I know this isn't helping, but it's a way for me to make my point by using someone else as an example.

"He acted like he didn't know me." Talie sobbed. "Do you know what he said?"

"What?"

"I said, 'Frank, it's me,' and do you know what he said?"

I couldn't guess.

"He said, 'We're not interested,' and hung up."

"That's rotten," I say.

"You know what? I heard his wife in the background," Talie says. "He *is* married."

I couldn't say "Of course he is"—if it were anyone else, I would've, I might've thrown a dismissive wave of my hand for good measure. But Talie says it as if she were just learning of the possibility, and when this innocence washes up on the shore of her cheeks, I just want to stand there and wade in it.

"Have you been inside yet?" I ask. Slow, lyricless music plays in the ballroom at the end of the carpeted hall.

"I can't go in without a date," she says, and without asking me, I know what this means.

"It would be my pleasure," I say, holding my arm out in an exaggerated way.

"Tuck in your shirt," Talie says, pointing.

I shove the ends of the collarless shirt I threw on into my jeans.

"That's better," Talie says, and takes up my arm. "Let's do this thing."

If I live to be one million, I know I won't forget how it feels to stroll through the doors of the ballroom into the garden of sound where couples are waltzing elegantly on the shiny marble dance floor. Talie has those little ways of making you want her, like every woman does, the way she might look at you and make you feel like you are extraordinary when you need it, the way she revolves on the outside of group conversations, like she used to do in high school when we were kids, giving me that anxiety where I was afraid the rope would snap and she'd float into a new orbit and out of mine for good.

Talie scowls at anyone who dares to point out my informal dress. We waltz on the outside corner of the dance floor, and Talie stares straight into me as she waltzes us toward the center of the floor, where we turn and turn among the staring.

"Who do you know here?" I ask.

"There are some girls from my cotillion class," Talie says. "I don't want to talk to them, though. I told them all about Dale—showed them a picture, if you can believe that—and they're probably wondering who you are."

"It seems like there are a lot of couples here," I say.

Talie continues to waltz me in time to the music.

"All these chicks have boyfriends," Talie says bitterly. "They think this is the fucking prom or something."

"Why didn't Dale come tonight?" I ask, suddenly curious.

"You know," Talie says. "He had things to do."

The waltz ends and the eager couples wait for the next song as Talie and I exit the dance floor.

Talie slumps down in a chair at a fully set table and I slip into the chair next to her.

"I just wanted to dance one dance," Talie says.

"I'll stay as long as you want," I tell her. "Do you want me to get you anything?"

"There was supposed to be dinner . . . but it looks like we missed it."

"Where's the bar?" I ask, looking around.

Talie laughs. "You and I are probably the only ones of age here."

"Really?"

"Most of the girls in my class are still in high school," Talie says. She sighs. "I wish I would've learned at that age what they're learning now. It might've made a difference."

I touch Talie on the knee but self-consciously withdraw my hand when a couple passes our table.

"Which fork is this?" I ask.

"Salad," Talie answers automatically, like a game show contestant.

"I used to think the different sizes were for different-size hands," I admit.

Either Frank tells fantastic tales or Talie translates them through a distorted lens, because the description Talie gave when I asked where Frank lived doesn't match the address we pull in front of. Where Talie said "huge Tudor manor" I would say "ranch house."

"Is this it?" I ask.

"Yep," Talie giggles. "Are we really going to do this?"

The question didn't come up in the grocery store where we bought the toilet paper and gallon of vinegar. The vinegar was my idea, and when I see the speedboat parked in Frank's driveway, I know it was the right choice. "Why not?" I say. Talie giggles again and her smile makes me happy.

"This is *so* juvenile," she says before opening the car door.

Frank's front yard is treeless, so we sneak right up to the house.

"Go around back and I'll toss you one," I tell Talie. She nods and her cotillion dress glows in the night. As she disappears behind the darkened house, I unscrew the vinegar and climb aboard the boat. I unzip the plastic seat covers and soak the seat cushions with vinegar. A sharp odor rises and I stand back, spilling vinegar on my shoes. I roll the plastic bottle along the bow, and it comes to rest against a guardrail, empty.

I hop down and unwrap the toilet paper, launching a roll over the house. A thin white stripe hangs over the front of the house. A few seconds pass and the roll comes back over, bouncing off the slanted roof. I can hear Talie laughing in the backyard, and when we're out of toilet paper, the front of the house looks like a giant face with white bangs in its eyes.

I find Talie in the backyard, staring at a tree swing.

"His daughter is adorable," Talie whispers. She gives the swing a little push. "You should see how cute she is."

"We should go," I tell her. "We made a lot of noise."

I tug on Talie's dress and we walk silently across the lawn. As we pull away, Talie looks back for something and I look up in the rearview mirror, but all I see is a house where Talie wishes she lived. A light comes on for a moment in one of the upper windows and then goes out again. The smell of vinegar from my shoes makes Talie roll down the window, and she leans her seat back, silent as I drive us home in the moonless night.

Essay #9: A Nightmarish Day

Here is the worst possible scenario in my life:

I fall in love, get married, live in bliss, have children, get a job with regular hours, watch my children grow up and drift away, lose interest in my wife, cheat on her with prostitutes who don't satisfy me, lose interest in life altogether, kill myself.

I Give a Lift

The more I am kept waiting by the police, the more comical Dale's phone call seems.

"*Please* hurry up," he begged, as if he were going somewhere. "And don't tell *anyone.*" I knew he meant Talie, but the thought that I would hang up the phone and turn to anyone and say, "My best friend's boyfriend just got arrested for soliciting an undercover cop," is like the punch line of a really bad joke.

Curious choice, calling me, is what I'm thinking. Before I even find out the details, I know I will use this to blackmail Dale out of our lives forever.

I don't bother to let Dale tell his story in the car. "How are you going to keep this from Talie?" is all I ask.

"She doesn't know what goes on with me," Dale says with mock bravura, then, gloomily, "They impounded my car. I'll have to tell her it's in the shop."

I'm silent, letting him know I won't help him in any way whatsoever.

"Should I pull up or let you off down the street?" I ask. "Talie left Arrowhead Ranch around four, and I'm sure she's wondering why you're not home."

"Go around the block," Dale instructs, his voice full of alarm. "I've got to get it together."

Dale's suit looks damp, giving the impression that he has just come in from the rain. His tie is gone, probably balled up in his pocket, and his jacket smells distinctly of being somewhere he shouldn't have been. I tell Dale this and he takes his jacket off, folds it over his arm.

"All I want to know is, have you done this before while dating Talie?" I say.

Dale doesn't look at me, doesn't even try to hold me with an honest stare when he says, "No, this is the only time."

I sense true confession and pull over, letting Dale out.

"Okay, thanks," he says, worriedly looking down the street in the direction of his house. "On second thought, could you come in? I'll tell her you gave me a ride from the shop."

I consider my obligations here.

I think of things I'd rather be doing.

"Sure," I agree.

Talie isn't in the lit house and there's no note, but Dale rockets into the bathroom and showers without really calling for her. I snap the TV on and sit on the couch, which is warm and recently abandoned. Something pulls me to the window and I see Talie walking away from a car that takes off in the opposite direction.

"Hi," I greet her at the back door.

"Tell him you found me outside," she says, leading me back to the front room.

We snuggle together on the couch, her excited body vibrating next to me. I put my arm around her and she wilts against me. The perfume of her hair is intoxicating and I'm facedown drunk when the shower stops.

The bathroom door cracks and we break apart.

"There you are, honey," Dale calls out.

"Found her in the backyard," I say.

"Let me get dressed," he says. A door slams.

"Let him get dressed," Talie repeats, smiling at me.

Journal #9

"'Cheese' on three," Jenny's mother says. "One, two, three." The camera snaps and Jenny giggles as we blink away the flash.

"Should we go?" I ask, admiring Jenny's turquoise prom dress.

"Haven't you forgotten something?" Jenny asks.

I'm thinking: hotel room, limo, liquor, two cigarettes, box of condoms, the list completed by the mad scramble to find someone in the parking lot of the 7-Eleven to buy the liter of Franzia. I shrug and Jenny smiles, clears her throat, and touches a strap on her dress.

"Oh," I say. "Yeah, hold on."

Jenny and her mother laugh as I jump down the hall to the kitchen to retrieve Jenny's corsage.

"'Cheese' on three," Jenny's mother says after five minutes of my fumbling with the corsage, before Jenny recognizes that I accidentally bought a wrist corsage.

The flash pops, waving Jenny and me into the final lap of our master plan, a night we've been planning since her mother agreed that Jenny could attend the prom at Randolph. So many late nights on the sectional in front of an unwatched movie ending in "Let's wait," so many aborted gropes in the steamed-up front seat of my car.

The last of the day's sun colors a stripe of orange across Jenny's forehead as I shut the door for her, then skip around to the driver's side. I speed down the freeway toward the parking lot of the Marriott, where our limo awaits—Jenny knew her mother would add two and two if I picked her up in a limo, but I fought for the extravagance and persuaded Jenny to lie to her mother, something she'd never done.

"I still feel guilty," Jenny says.

"It's not too late to call off the limo," I say, a little game we've been playing that up until now has given us some measure of power in the matter. We both know that power is gone now.

"I love you," Jenny says, not as a way to end the conversation, or make it veer, but because it's just something we say, and lately it's the only thing that comes out of my mouth that makes any sense to me: "I love you, too," I say.

"Slow down," Jenny says. "We've got all of our lives. Unless you kill us with your driving." She looks over at me and smiles, remembers my joke about how we're like old people, a sentiment echoed by our friends, and I almost don't look at the road again, caught by the way Jenny looks at me, which makes me feel loved, a look that makes me feel like I'm more than I know I really am.

We exchange my car for the silver stretch in the Marriott parking lot. The chauffeur opens the door for us and we feel like royalty. I point out our hotel room through the moonroof as the limo glides out of the parking lot. A shiver runs through Jenny and she says, "I can't wait." She slides her hand inside my purple paisley cummerbund, teasing.

"We could just skip the dance," I suggest casually.

Jenny pulls back in mock horror. "No we can't!"

"We'll see after a few drinks at Octavio's," I say slyly, kidding.

"I left the fake ID in my other purse," Jenny says, startled. "Oh no, I've ruined it."

I shrug dramatically. She could've told me the limo had sunk to the bottom of the ocean, the driver killed instantly, the windows sealed, and I would've assured her it was no problem, a minor inconvenience, a trifling.

"Actually, Mario got fired," I tell her, almost forgetting. "But he's going to have someone from the kitchen stash the bottle in the limo while we're eating."

"Genius," Jenny says admiringly. "It might've been a little obvious, what with you in a tux, and this." She rotates the corsage on her wrist.

"Yeah," I agree, "and I doubt there'll be any other prommies at Octavio's. So it'll be like eating in a fish bowl."

Jenny smiles deviously. "Got an idea."

I smile back. "Yeah?"

"Let's order in."

That's my Jenny. Bold and daring.

"Can we?"

"Don't know why not," I say.

Plates clank around our feet as the chauffer opens the door. Jenny passes me the bottle of yellow-label brut and I finish it, the bubbles swarming in my head. Our chauffer says he'll return the plates and silverware to Octavio's, and I reach into my wallet and pull out a twenty. "Here," I say. "Give this to the guy in the kitchen, would ya?" The chauffer looks at the bill with disdain and then snaps it up. Jenny laughs and we both know the guy in the kitchen will never see the Jackson.

Stepping through the Randolph gymnasium doors, our names ringing in our ears, is like stepping through a portal in time: The walls are papered black, and silver foil streamers float magically through the air, colliding now and again with the silver, white, and black helium balloons hammering away at the ceiling of the illuminated tent anchored in the middle of the floor, the basketball hoops at either end of the floor hoisted up toward the ceiling to make way.

A slow song starts and I grab Jenny up, pressing her dangerously close, a violation surely to bring one of the chaperones. Jenny wriggles some space between us and I spot Jason and his girlfriend, Sally, twirling under a silver banner.

"My head feels like one of those balloons," Jenny says. We sway in time to the song we've made out to many times before, the saccharine words carrying a tinge of weight on this particular night. "Did I thank you for dinner?" Jenny asks.

"Yes, you did," I say.

"Well, thank you again."

"You're welcome again," I say, spinning her. Our forward progress stops and we twirl slowly in a circle, my rented shoes scuffing arcs in the polished floor.

"Are you ready to leave?" Jenny asks.

"I don't know. Are you?"

"I think I am."

A nervous excitement grips me. Earlier, in front of the mirror, there was still the limo to pick up, the hotel key to get, dinner, the dance itself. A song Jenny and I agree we don't like starts up and I say, "I'm ready if you are."

"Think the limo is back?" Jenny asks.

I look at Jenny to see if she's stalling, and see that she's looking back at me in the same way, to see if I'll use the excuse of waiting for the limo to put it off a little longer, which I almost do, reminiscing about the last dance, knowing that once we leave the gymnasium, the prom will be just a memory, but I don't want to send the wrong signal, so I say, "I'll have a friend drop us off."

It isn't until Jenny and I stumble out of Jason's car—the object of Jason and Sally's jokes all the way to the hotel—that we realize we weren't ready to leave. We realize it after we've opened the box of Franzia and kissed drunken kisses, doing everything we've done before, just up and until, our prom outfits laid out neatly, a stall we didn't recognize. Jenny comes back from the bathroom and we laugh at our naked selves, telling each other it's okay, that we've got all our lives.

A Friend of the Groom's

The grass JSB has rolled across the desert landscaping gives the grounds a lush, fertile feel. Everything seems to be growing and alive. Wedding guests mill around the pool, up near the house, next to the bar set up on the patio of the guesthouse. Talie is standing near JSB's rose garden, talking to Peters from legal. I wave and they wave back.

The caterers are clanging around in the kitchen, stacking trays of food in tall metal containers to keep it warm until the ceremony ends. I run my finger into a cream-filled pastry and no one sees me.

The door to JSB's room is closed, so I knock before letting myself in.

"Charlie," he says when he sees me. His shirt is unbuttoned and he's collapsed on the couch at the foot of his bed. "Come in."

He offers me a drink and I say no thanks.

Erin comes out of the bathroom in her wedding gown, and she's so beautiful I forget who I am. "You look fantastic," I say, kissing her on the cheek.

"Thanks," she says. She models the dress.

"That was Talie's mother's wedding dress," JSB says from the couch.

The image of JSB in the bedroom at the suite at the Pointe South Mountain Resort flickers suddenly and I say, "What?"

"Her mother wore that dress on her wedding day," he says. He gestures toward Erin like a tour guide and my eyes follow, tracing the white silk down the curves of Erin's body—Erin, who wasn't even born when Talie's mother married JSB. I want to burn the dress while Erin's wearing it. I want to splash a bucket of acid on her and watch the dress and her skin melt away.

I can't spit out any words.

"Charlie, I know we don't really know each other," Erin starts. I think she's actually going to reach out and put her arm around me, so I take a step backward. "But we're like a family now, and—"

"We *are* a family," JSB says, standing. He poses the three of us together in the full-length mirror, him in the middle, his right hand—the one he probably used either to hold down or to guide himself into Kiki—hangs over my shoulder. "One big, happy family," he says.

Erin giggles.

"I should find Talie," I say, loosening myself from the weight of JSB's arm. "It's your happy day," I say as I walk out. "It's your hap-hap-happy day."

A woman with chocolaty brown hair is admiring the hand-carved antique grandfather clock in the hall when I slam the door to JSB's bedroom.

"God, you scared me," she says, putting her hand across her chest.

I'm not even going to say sorry, I think, but the sight of her seems to calm me and I introduce myself.

"Caitlin," she says. "I work for JSB."

"Oh," I say.

Caitlin, it turns out, is twenty-eight and is the new salesperson hired specifically to champion the new line of cosmetics.

"That's a big deal," I say. Caitlin leans toward me aggressively, and I lean forward, meeting her gaze. She talks about her upcoming trip—New York, Boston, and Montreal—and about how the new products are going to make Buckley a leader in the industry. She uses phrases like "leader in the industry."

I tell her I'm in charge of the promotional contest. I tell her I've named the contest World Gone Water.

"Oh," she says, nodding in a way that suggests she's heard of me, or knows who I am, and I begin to panic. The walls of JSB's estate feel like prison, and the feeling of being stared at and recognized comes over me. I take Caitlin out a sliding glass door on the side of the house and we pass Talie on the walkway. I introduce them. I notice a faint bruise on Talie's neck.

"Where's Dale?" I ask.

"He's here," she says. "Somewhere."

Talie winks and waltzes off.

Caitlin and I walk to the front lawn, where most of the wedding party has assembled. JSB motions for me to come stand next to him.

"Save me a dance," Caitlin says, smiling.

I take my place next to JSB, across from Talie, who is in Erin's line (at JSB's insistence), and Talie rolls her eyes at me.

The organist under the white canopy begins and everyone rises, and Caitlin stands last, making sure I am watching. As Erin passes down the aisle, my gaze lifts from the veiled stranger to Caitlin, whose smile reaches all the way to the back of me.

"It was lovely," everyone says at one point or another during the reception.

Caitlin dances with other men to make me jealous, so I take Gayle Witherspoon, a secretary from legal, and waltz her around the dance floor. A noxious force field of perfume prevents me from really holding Gayle tight, but Caitlin gets the message and rubs up against me after the song ends. I release Gayle and she stumbles awkwardly off the dance floor.

"Does the best man have to stay all night?" Caitlin asks.

A Romantic Interlude

Caitlin brings me back to her room at the Arizona Biltmore Hotel, a cabana near the main pool. The light coming from the pool is webbed on the walls of the cabanas, and the waves from a couple splashing each other in the shallow end send the light into motion, creating the effect of weak lightning. I have trouble keeping my balance when I stare straight down into the pool.

"Come on," Caitlin says from behind me. She's hiding behind the windowed double doors and I can see her nude body through the white curtains. As I reach the door, the pool light goes out and the splashing in the pool quiets. In the absence of the pool light, the moon switches on and Caitlin's skin glows under my fingers.

Unbelievably, there isn't a test to pass before I'm allowed to touch Caitlin.

"We have what no one else does," I'd have to say to Jane.

Caitlin makes me forget about Jane.

And everyone that's ever come before her.

Curiosity overtakes me when we're lying in bed. I can't stop looking at her. I have to kiss her every five minutes. I touch her body with my lips to make sure she is real.

"You're doing something strange to me," Caitlin says, putting her hand over her heart.

"Do you feel it too?" I ask, placing my hand on hers.

"I'll have to be careful you don't capture my heart," she says, giggling. She rolls on top of me and the warm press of her skin undoes me.

Under her spell, I play a game of nude chess with her on the giant lawn chess board on the hotel grounds. Caitlin knocks one of the rooks down and lies on the grassy square. "Come capture it," she says, sprawling out.

In the morning, robed and having breakfast at the tiny table outside her cabana, she looks at me and asks, "How long have I known you?"

"It feels like forever," I say, getting up to kiss her.

Caitlin decides she wants me to come along on her sales trip, and I decide I can get away with saying I'm doing work for the contest, so I leave a message on Talie's machine and meet Caitlin at the airport for the flight to New York City. One of those chiseled-jaw guys is across the aisle from us in first class, and Caitlin makes a comment about him, purring a little, and I'm surprised at how much it burns me, how much it makes me want to pop the window with this guy's head, exposing the whole cabin to a loss of pressure, everyone being sucked out over Kansas. "Oh yeah?" I say, and, sensing I am upset, Caitlin says, "It doesn't mean he has my heart."

"Who has it?" I ask, wanting to hear it. Caitlin touches her finger to my chest and I kiss her in front of the chiseled-jaw guy to let him know what he'll never have.

What we see of New York: We start at the zoo in Central Park, as it's right outside the Plaza Hotel, our digs (we don't pay to go in the zoo, just look over the fence while the sea lions are being fed). I ride my hand up Caitlin's dress when she's leaned over the zoo fence. People are cramming on all sides but no one sees me, and I slip my finger inside her and I think maybe the guy next to us hears her gasp.

We retrace our steps to the Plaza, and once we're clear of the chandeliers and lunch crowd, she pushes me against the inside of the elevator and rips my shirt clean open, the tiny white plastic buttons scattering around us.

Later, I ask if I can take her out to dinner. I'd like to get dressed up, see her across a candlelit table. The fantasy is ruined, though, when Caitlin says, "Dinner's right here"—a line from a thousand porno movies—and puts her hand between my legs. She takes me in her mouth and I remember when Jason and I used to call each other by our porno names. We followed the rule of taking the name of the street where you lived as your last name. I was Charlie Olive and he was Jason Greenwich.

We used our porno names once, I almost forgot, when we met these two sisters in Las Vegas:

"Let's go inside," the tall, blond, big-nosed girl said as she stood up.

"Help me up," I said. I had about twenty gallons of alcohol inside me and I looked down her inclined driveway at the gate, which was just closing.

"Hey," Jason greeted us. He was sitting next to our good friend who'd moved to Las Vegas for the luck, and with them was the tall, blond, big-nosed girl's sister.

"Wanna hit?" Jason asked.

I pushed the joint away.

"Let's all climb in your bed," the tall, blond, big-nosed girl suggested to her sister.

"Great idea," her sister agreed.

Suddenly the five of us were underneath the covers, passing around a chilled bottle of Southern Comfort. (The sister claimed it tasted better cold.) I looked over at my good friend who'd moved to Las Vegas for the luck and saw him kissing the tall, blond, big-nosed girl's sister.

"Go get it, girl," the blond big-nose whooped.

"Shh!" the sister warned. "The housekeeper is sleeping."

"The housekeeper?" I asked.

"Don't worry, she's old," the blond big-nose muttered.

"When are your parents coming back?" Jason asked.

"End of the week," the blond big-nose answered as she took a swig from the now half-empty bottle. "Fuck!"

"What?" I asked.

"I forgot to turn the lights off in the driveway," she said, and sprang off the mattress.

"I'll go with you," I called out after her, and stumbled from the bed.

The hallway was dark and I heard her flicking light switches off. Then she came back up the hall.

"Wait," I said, and pulled her up against me. We started kissing and I put my hand up her shirt and massaged her breasts. She started getting into it, so I reached down her underwear.

"We can't now," she whispered as she pulled my hand out from between her legs.

"I want you now," I said, and lunged at her.

"Hold on." She stopped me.

"Till when?"

"Later," she whispered loudly. "In my room."

"Okay," I agreed, following her back into the bedroom, where the others were still lounging.

"How often do you guys come to Vegas?" the tall, blond, big-nosed girl's sister asked us.

"Not enough," Jason said. A real cheese machine.

I reached under the covers, hoping to get my hands in the tall, blond, big-nosed girl's crotch again, but when I felt down there, I found Jason had beaten me to the prize.

"Go with me to the fridge," the blond big-nose said to him, and the two of them leaped out of bed.

By the time I stumbled after them, they'd already gone into her bedroom. I crept up to the door and listened.

"Let me get a rubber," I heard her say.

"I brought one," Jason said.

"Oh?"

"Never can tell what you're going to run into in Sin City," the cheese machine said.

Oh my God, I was thinking.

He started giving it to her, because she moaned a few low moans and then squealed a little.

"Hey," I said as I walked in.

Suddenly everything was silent. It was so dark I couldn't even make out the bed. I stood there for a minute, hoping to be invited into a threesome, but no one said anything. I quietly closed the door behind me.

I walked back to the sister's bedroom and opened the door. Our good friend from Las Vegas had the sister spread out naked on the bed and was licking between her legs. She looked over and smiled at me and I closed the door.

I was starting to sober up and I didn't like what was going on. I felt what it was like to lose out on something because I wasn't man enough to just take it. I went out into the front room and sulked on the couch, trying to explain to the housekeeper who I was.

In the morning, while Caitlin is with a client, I skip down Fifth Avenue to a bagel cart for some breakfast. A swell of people come out from the subway under the Plaza, everyone in a business suit or dark clothes. I skip back up the Plaza's steps, palming a warm cinnamon raisin bagel, skip past a limousine with its door opening and past a family of tourists gawking at the chandeliers.

**

In Boston, Caitlin and I have a terrible fight on Lansdowne Street. The fight starts in Axis, where we came to dance. "I'm too tired to dance," Caitlin says. "Let's go somewhere else."

Thinking she really wants a good time, I take the lead and force her on the dance floor. She gyrates lethargically in place to the bass beat of an unrecognizable song before turning and walking off the dance floor.

The fight continues in Jillian's, a pool hall down the street.

"You are *insensitive*," she says. "It's amazing what you can find out about a person."

"Let's just go back to the hotel, okay?" I say. Her insults are mortally wounding me.

I sleep fitfully on the floor, dreaming a dream where Caitlin is riding in a horse-drawn carriage through Central Park while I am running after her on foot. I am calling out to her, but when she looks back, her carriage takes off into the air, gliding over the park and into the clouds. When I try to show someone a picture of Caitlin to find out where she's gone, I realize I don't have any. When I try to pronounce her name to the police, it's untranslatable by the cop.

In the morning I wake when Caitlin crawls down on the floor too. "I'm sorry," I say, hoping today is a new day.

"I'm the one that's sorry," she says.

Our breath is foul when we kiss, but neither of us flinches, and Caitlin says, "I have the weekend off. Let's take a car trip."

"I asked the guy at the counter for a romantic place, and he said there's something called the Colonial Inn in Concord. I guess it's supposed to be historic," I say.

"Well, well," Caitlin says, chuckling. "Aren't we a little Romeo?"

"It sounded like a place that might be haunted, though," I say, ignoring her.

"We could go there," she says, kissing my neck. "Or we could go to Cape Cod."

"Why did you say that just now? The Romeo thing," I ask, pulling away.

"I don't know," she answers, shrugging. "I just thought it was cute that you were, you know . . . doing *research*."

"You were being condescending," I say. I know what kind of reaction this'll get.

Caitlin is silent, then says in a quiet voice, "I'm sorry."

I'm surprised that I have her on the fence. I feel like pushing her further. "Are you a condescending person?" I ask.

Caitlin sits back and closes her eyes. She begins to tremble.

"Look, I was only joking," I say, not surprised at how quickly I back off. "I know you're a good person."

My words have no visible effect on her and I'm stuck for what to say next.

Instead, Caitlin says, "I have this terrible feeling that I'm in love with you."

"Why is that such a terrible thing?"

Caitlin stands, not looking at me, and says, "It really feels great, but I have to guard against it. You're not going to be around forever."

The last words sear me completely.

"I *will* be here forever," I want to say. And even though I *think* it's true, it would sound corny and melodramatic after knowing her for only a few days, so I don't say anything, and we move silently to pack our bag for the weekend.

Things are as they were, though, once we're driving toward the Cape. Caitlin touches the inside of my thigh while I drive, and I glance over and catch her smile.

A giant yellow wreath hangs on the bridge over the canal we cross to get onto the Cape, marking the spot where a woman drove head-on into a metal pole, killed on impact. It was on the news the night before in the hotel, and what occurs to me is that forty-eight hours ago at this time, that person was alive and making plans to drive to the Cape, along with whatever else she was doing that day, picking up laundry, paying her electric bill, calling her friends to say she was on her way.

There was a girl who got killed when I first moved to Phoenix, a foreign exchange student from Russia who stepped out in front of a city bus while looking the wrong way. They put her picture in the newspaper, along with one of a makeshift memorial featuring flowers and a teddy bear that sprang up at the site of the accident. I couldn't look away from the picture. I somehow knew the confusion from that morning, the chaos of running late and the nanosecond that was nothing more than a mistake that cost this girl her life.

The windows on the rental car are manual, so Caitlin climbs in the backseat to unroll them. The wind coming off the ocean scrubs everything clean, and you get a new life.

"I'm just going to sit back here," Caitlin says.

"But I want you up here," I say, patting the seat next to me, looking in the rearview mirror.

"Nope." She smiles. "I'm going to sit back here."

"What'll you do by yourself back there?" I ask.

I love to be coy with her.

"I'm going to put my feet up on your shoulders and masturbate. Will you keep the speed above sixty?"

I eye her in the mirror. "Someone will see," I say, even though I wouldn't care if someone did. It simply seems to me that we could have a nice drive on Cape Cod, squeezed on all sides by ocean and sand, and enjoy ourselves in this pacific freedom without starring in a porn movie. "Come back up front," I say, more telling her than asking.

Caitlin puts on a pout and climbs over the front seat. She turns the radio on and a moment of total division passes between us.

"I wasn't going to do that anyway," she says apologetically. "I was only joking."

"It's a nice day, isn't it?" I ask.

Caitlin rests her head on my lap and closes her eyes. "It *is* a nice day," she says.

An old drive-in movie sign in Wellfleet makes me think of a hundred things from high school.

The Cape narrows, and soon there's beach and ocean visible in every direction. The wind becomes fierce, and Caitlin, sensing something, sits up.

"We've driven to the end," I say. "I didn't even notice."

Caitlin points out the sign for Race Point Beach and I pull off. THIS BEACH CLOSES AT DARK, the sign says. Except for a family wading down the shore, the beach is deserted. The showers in the changing room drip synchronically, and the sandy slope down to the water is one of the walks you know is going to be harder on the way back up.

"Bury me in the sand," Caitlin says.

I kick away the dry sand and scoop handfuls of thick, wet sand onto her body, packing it on tight. Caitlin giggles as I do, and I shape two giant breasts out of sand and put a large tangle of seaweed between her legs.

"Is that what you really want?" Caitlin asks, looking down at her mountainous breasts.

"I want what's inside," I tell her.

Caitlin smiles. "I'm trapped here."

"Yes, you are."

The rest of the afternoon floats away on the open water. The sun takes a last breath and goes under, darkening the water until the ocean is heard more than it is seen.

"I love you," I say to Caitlin.

"You are making me crazy," she says, and the way she looks at me, everything inside her collapsing at once, lets me know that that was the reason I was put on this earth and that she's glad she finally found me.

"I can't believe I finally found someone like you," I say.

We kiss until a spotlight lights us up and we're told to leave.

"Do you want to drive into Provincetown for dinner?" I ask.

"We should probably check into a motel first," she says.

I know once we get to the motel, we probably won't leave, that Caitlin will order room service, or order a pizza, and sure enough, she plops onto the blue floral bedspread in a way that lets me know she's in for the night.

"Come over here," she says, lifting her arms.

"Let me take you out tonight," I say. "There's probably a ton of great places to eat right off the beach."

The minute the words leave my mouth, I want to get them all back.

"There's a great place to eat right here," she says, spreading her legs wide. There's a second where I can turn it into something funny, where I can make a joke or a retort, but while my hope that she will quit saying things like that in favor of something sexier and more romantic is being dashed, I miss it.

I do not what I want to do, but what I feel like I am required to do, until the ugly confidence comes back into Caitlin and she rolls away and turns out the light. Outside, the ocean could be a million miles away.

Caitlin's meeting in Montreal is off Sainte-Catherine, so I wait across the street in a café where no one is smoking but everyone seems to want to. Montreal is our last destination and things between me and Caitlin are shifting. She's holding back now, not telling me she loves me, not holding my hand. "Decompressing" is what she calls it.

I try to picture Phoenix again, and it's such a former life that I won't be able to name things I see once we land. My grand plan (the new one) is to put my offer on the table: I'll do anything to be with her. We could live the way we've been living, hotels and new cities. I think Caitlin just needs someone to make the move, and the idea thrills me.

I'm still pretty jacked up about it later at dinner and it's all I can do to keep from spitting it out.

Outside the restaurant window, Notre-Dame lights up dramatically and Caitlin turns to see it.

"That's beautiful," she says.

"I don't care much for churches," I tell her.

"Me neither," she says. "But it looks impressive."

"You don't have a religion?" I ask.

She shakes her head no. "Don't need it."

I jump up and reach for her hand. She looks around wildly and then looks at me, pulling back. "I think we should be together," I say.

"We are together," she says, straightening her napkin in her lap.

"No, I mean I think we should try and . . ." I'm at a loss for what to call it. "You know, I love you and—"

"Charlie, stop," she says.

The whole moment is flushed away just like that. The waiter comes to take our order and Caitlin waves him away.

The jet lag from Phoenix to New York to Boston to Montreal kicks in, and all the organs inside me collapse, my veins narrowing until the air burns in my lungs. "Do you love me?" I ask.

Caitlin looks away, wanting the waiter to come back. "It doesn't matter," she says.

"Doesn't matter how?"

"Please don't do this," she begs. "This is our last weekend together and we've been having a great time."

"*You've* been having a great time," I correct her. "It really isn't a great time having your heart broken." The words "heart broken" hit her like an oncoming truck.

"What do you want me to do?" she asks, crying a little, which pacifies me in some way. "I can't give myself completely over. I've done that too many times and it never works out."

"It can work out with us," I say.

"That's the first thing all of them said too," she says, composing herself.

"Yeah, but this time will be different."

"That's the next thing they said," she says coldly.

"I'm starting to see your point," I say. I throw my napkin on the table. I play my last card: "Maybe it's *not* worth it."

Caitlin wants to disagree, I can physically feel the pull inside of her, see it in her expression. But she wins out over it and looks right into me and says, "I just can't."

The restaurant in Montreal feels like an outpost on a dream map and I wish I could close my eyes and transport myself.

"Where's the waiter?" Caitlin asks.

"You sent him away, remember? You think he's going to rush right back?"

"Don't get that way," she warns. "Let's try to have a nice meal."

"I'm not hungry," I say. "I'll see you back at the hotel."

I walk out, passing the waiter on his way to the kitchen, and the two of us take a few steps in the same direction, walking like Siamese twins. "She knows what she wants," I tell him.

Paroled into the cold night, I head in the direction of Notre-Dame. The shadows vibrate on the pavement and I start to think about how Caitlin is right. Why give yourself up to someone fully?

I was sitting there trying to deny what I knew was true. Months from now I'd be tired of her, or she'd be tired of me, the excitement of newness worn and forgotten.

I tell her she's right when she gets back to the hotel. "You were totally right," I say. "I don't know what I was thinking."

"Who's she?" Caitlin asks, pointing at the redheaded hooker in the bed next to me, who is rolling a joint.

"It's Diedre, right?" I ask the hooker. Diedre nods. "This is Diedre," I tell Caitlin.

"Nice to meet you," Diedre says without looking away from the joint.

If I hear what I think I hear—Caitlin crying in the hallway, stomping down to the elevator—it doesn't faze me one iota, and Caitlin can take her traveling act to California, for all I care.

Dr. Hatch,

Remember what you said about how the thing that affects your life the most—death—doesn't hardly involve you in any way? Remember I said how it affects other people's lives and we talked about my parents, about the vacuum of nothing I was sucked into when they died? I'm writing to you from there again.

The love of my life is dead. You never met Talie, but she came to see me a couple of times at SRC. It was her slut friend, Holly, who got her killed. I don't think I've ever mentioned Holly to you and I'm not going to start now. Talie was always getting into trouble with Holly, and this time it wasn't trouble I could get her out of. The police found them both in a Dumpster with their clothes torn off.

The funeral was at Saint Francis Xavier, the church adjacent to my old school, Randolph College Prep. The only people who came to the funeral were her foster parents, her biological father, me, and the boyfriend I'm sure she was going to leave.

I stayed after everyone was gone to be alone with Talie one last time. I wanted to open the casket and see her again, have her pop up and say, "Let's go." I feel completely untethered without her. You never know how much you need someone until, well, you know.

I used to tell Talie I was going to go to Europe, that I was going to fly away and shed everything anyone ever knew about me and everything that was in my past. Whenever I told her about moving to Europe, she would say, "The unknown is more frightening than what you know, no matter how shitty what you know is." The unknown is what there is to fear, she would say, and the future is definitely unknown. I told her I feared my *past*. But it isn't so much that I fear what I have done, but I fear I am missing some vital component—the gene that makes you walk on green and stop on red, the thing that tells what the difference between red and green even is. My fear isn't of my future; it's that my past lives there, happily, shimmering in the warmth it creates, perpetuating the voice that assures me, *It's all right, it's okay.*

I'm feeling the same sense of loss I felt when I told Karine I was sorry. She came to see me before she disappeared (I know you're dying to hear me talk about this, so here it is), and we sat and did a crossword puzzle. I used a blue pen and she used pink so that when the puzzle was solved, we'd know who did what.

I told Karine I was sorry and she looked across the metal table at me and said, "I forgive you."

Right there, at the metal table, a half-finished crossword puzzle between us, I realized how much I'd lost in life. When I said I was sorry, it started in my mind as a casual thing to say. But when Karine looked at me like she did and said she forgave me, I knew she had been waiting to hear me say it, and I realized that what I had done to her was the biggest loss in her life.

It made me think about my own loss and I saw myself as something small and stupid, with a grin of infinite hope on my face.

Some people just don't get the chance to live in the world.

Talie never got a start, and everyone I know—including me—is to blame.

After the hearse became a black dot on the road, me promising to catch up, I crossed the lawn to Randolph Prep. William Randolph, the school's founder, died at sea. I used to stare at the portrait of him in the main hall, standing on the bow of a ship, maybe the one he went down on, straining to peer so far into the distance, maybe looking for what sailing would lead him to next.

"A banker by profession, Randolph was an avid sailor, captaining many voyages around the world," read the engraving under the portrait.

Details of his death weren't dramatic enough to reach the status of legend. Simply put, he was hit in the head when a sudden wind swung the sail into him. Randolph and his crew were one full day of sailing away from the shore. The banker/sailor never regained consciousness, and the exact moment of his death went unmarked by a dying word or wish for the world.

What a shock it must have been, the initial blow to Randolph's head, coming from his blind side. He probably never imagined he'd die while sailing, a sport at which he had become accomplished.

In my mind I tried to trace it back, not a straight line between Randolph's death in the water and his birth, but I wondered at the steps between the two events. Fate is too easily made the usual suspect. William Randolph could've been killed in any number of ways: an automobile crash (at high speed, or by a careless driver), an airplane wreck, a gunshot (self-inflicted, or random, accidental fire), a heart attack (in his sleep, or while shopping for chocolate bars in the local grocery store)—all could be uselessly labeled fate.

What are probably the facts: Someone introduced William Randolph to sailing, he enjoyed it, and he was killed, accidentally.

But what I really used to wonder about when I stood in the main hall, and what I often think about, was how easily the chain could've been broken. William Randolph might not have met someone who could introduce him to sailing; he might not have enjoyed it, it might have made him so sick he swore never to leave land; sailing might have proven too difficult for Randolph to master. None of the steps that led to Randolph's death was a conscious decision to do this over that, but if just one thing had gone the other way, his story—his life—might have had a different ending.

World Gone Water

I find Dale at Max Maxwell's, the bar at the Phoenician supplying the beverage service for the World Gone Water party. An hour early and standing around the Mojave Ballroom, its taupe-colored walls producing their own kind of nauseating light, I decided a drink would calm my nervous stomach. I knew one drink might lead to two, three, or four, but the caterers, with their suspicious eyes, forced me out of the ballroom and down to Max Maxwell's.

Dale looks like he's been at the bar since Talie's funeral.

"Are you coming to the party?" I ask.

Dale sips weakly from a glass of bourbon. He looks at me through the mirror behind the bar and sips again. He closes his eyes, as if he's trying to circle the wagons around a thought, but when he looks up again, this time directly at me, his face is blank. "You should come," I say. "Talie was a part of Buckley and she'd want you to come."

My capacity to say things that may or may not be true has reached the level of artistry, and I feel the full force of this statement's design.

"Did I see you at her grave this morning?" Dale asks.

Suddenly I notice the grass stains on his knees, dirty green swatches painted on his suit pants.

"I am not particularly fond of you," I want to say to Dale. "Talie didn't love you," I want to say. "Talie was in love with someone else," I want to say. "I don't want you hanging out at Talie's grave," I want to say.

"I just got back from picking up the winner and her husband," I say.

"The winner?" Dale asks.

Just mentioning it to Dale brings my anxiety full circle, the anxiety I felt waiting in the ballroom for Carol Bandes, our winner, and her husband, Martin, to arrive, the result of what happened when I made the official gesture of picking her and her husband up at their house in Flagstaff by limo, taking them to a private jet, and flying them to Phoenix for her makeover and the party.

I want to tell Dale what happened, but then again I don't, and I let Dale's question float off into space. I decide to skip the drink. I want to skip the party, too. I'm not even sure that I'm *required* to show. I was only to be the agent who brought everything to a conclusion (as little as I had to do with that), but nothing was ever said of me seeing it through to the end.

When I emerge from Max Maxwell's, the sky is black. There is no trace of the sunset I missed, and the moon makes ghosts of the saguaros on Camelback Mountain.

As I walk back toward the ballroom, I can see where the resort backs into the mountain, where the cement ends and the rock begins. A rash of stars suddenly appears in the sky and everything glows for a moment, until my eyes adjust and all I see again is cement and rock.

A caravan of black limousines rolls past me to the chandeliered entrance of the Phoenician. Flashbulbs explode around the limos, making the night blacker. I feel like I'm hiding in the bushes as

I watch Belinda and Kyle and Alisha each step out of their own limousine. Jon isn't among the photographers but is at Alisha's side, holding her hand, waving at the camera like a movie star.

The Bandeses' limousine lumbers up the driveway toward the entrance. Dale suddenly appears, carelessly wandering in the flower beds. He trips and falls to his knees and I move to help him up, but when he sees me, he pulls a dirty pistol from his jacket pocket. The possibilities of just how badly this could end unfold and multiply.

"Dale, don't," I say, but even I am unconvinced by my words, and I'm thinking no matter how it does turn out, all I'll be reading about in tomorrow's paper is Dale. What won't be in the paper, though—the story worth telling—is what happened when I arrived at the Bandeses'.

The contest was rigged so that someone from Arizona would win, and Carol Bandes was the first name we drew from the mailed entries that qualified. I made the half-hour flight up from Phoenix in the Buckley Cosmetics private jet to pick up Carol and Martin. From the airfield, a limousine shuttled me into the trees, in the direction of the Grand Canyon. The San Francisco Peaks loomed in the sky above. The snowcaps reminded you that even though you could see them, they were somewhere else, in a different place than where you were.

At a certain point traffic thinned, so that the only cars on the highway were those loaded down with families and crammed floor-to-ceiling with camping gear and luggage. The limo driver, a thin, dark-haired man, announced the address as he turned at the wooden sign bearing the number of the Bandeses' house.

I presented a dozen roses to Mrs. Bandes when I told her she had won the Buckley Cosmetics World Gone Water contest. JSB had stressed the importance of surprising the contest winner, if only to prevent the winner from declining, which would be bad publicity.

"The what?" she asked, leaning forward, squinting. Her close-cropped blond hair hugged her small features, and her smallish frame seemed to be swallowed by the open space behind her.

"Your name was drawn as the winner," I repeated.

"But I didn't—" Just then a tall, severe-looking man covered the distance in the sparse front room to the front door in two or three steps.

"Can I help you?" he asked. He stood behind his wife, and the two of them made for an impressive couple.

I explained myself again, the look on Carol's face growing increasingly confused, until her husband said, "Oh, I entered you in the contest, honey. It seemed like a lark."

Carol's confusion was replaced by an uncomfortable look, and she peered over my shoulder at the silent limo in her driveway. Finally they invited me inside.

The wooden floor creaked a minuet as the three of us made our way to the couch. Carol took the roses from me and I explained the day's plan to her.

"I don't know if I'm up for the trip today," Carol said. "I had some things I was going to do. As a matter of fact, if you were thirty minutes later, you would've missed us entirely."

Carol shifted on the couch. The silence inside brought every noise from outside right into the amphitheater of their living room.

"If you don't want to go," her husband said, "you don't have to go. I just thought you might like it."

Carol shot him an incredulous look and he glanced down at his shoes.

"I'm sure they have an alternate," he said, looking at me.

"I think you might enjoy yourself," I said. There was no alternate and I could feel this whole thing slipping into disaster. The idea that winning the contest would be an imposition in someone's life hadn't occurred to me, and I was unprepared to make a persuasive argument against it. "A limo ride, a short flight to Phoenix, a party at the Phoenician. Not a bad way to spend a day."

"I don't fly at night," Carol said.

"We'll put you up at the Phoenician for the night," I said. "We want you to enjoy yourselves."

Carol looked at Martin. Martin smiled, and Carol shrugged and said, "Okay, let me change and we'll go."

"There'll be a makeover in Phoenix," I said, which came out sounding more offensive than a litany of profanity, but Carol understood my meaning and reappeared unchanged, a small bag in her hand.

Once we were riding back toward the Flagstaff airport, Carol and Martin relaxed and they seemed to become one person. They laughed about a neighbor who had cut a tree down onto his house, and Martin talked a little bit about his part-time job at Snowbowl, the ski resort nearby. Martin was retired from the railroad—he used to run the logging routes from Washington State to Montana—a business he said was "dying out." His hands were large and powerful, and I felt myself hiding my own under my legs on the seat.

Suddenly the limousine sputtered and lost power. The hum of the engine choked off and we glided slower and slower until the driver pulled off the road and we stopped.

Carol and Martin looked at me, and we waited for the driver to appear at our door.

"She quit," the driver said. "Could be the high altitude."

Martin looked skeptical. "It sounded like the alternator quit." He jumped out, and I felt inclined to follow him even though I knew nothing about engines and how they made a car run.

Martin lifted the hood and peered into the massive gray intestines underneath. He jiggled a few hoses and touched the metal of the engine. You got the sense you were watching a doctor diagnosing a patient. "It's not the alternator," Martin said. "I wonder how old the battery is."

We both looked up to hear the driver's response, but he was leaning on the passenger door, his head tucked away inside the limousine, talking to Carol. Martin scowled and suddenly it was like I wasn't there.

"Excuse me," Martin said.

The driver's head popped up.

"How old is this battery?" Martin asked.

The driver laughed. "I don't work on them. I just drive them." He grinned at his own cleverness.

Martin's voice lowered a full octave. "Do you have tools in the trunk?"

The driver unlocked the trunk and handed Martin a small, red plastic toolbox. The tools inside clanged against one another. The sound carried up the vacant highway.

I stood back to watch Martin operate, but the sound of the limo driver's voice chatting up Carol distracted us both, and the fact that the driver wasn't right there under the hood with us seemed like a fist that just kept pounding and pounding. The driver's voice grew louder as he laughed at something he'd said. His voice took the high, nervous tone of bar talk, and Martin started tapping a wrench against the metal engine housing. The tapping started intermittently and grew louder until the driver looked over in our direction.

I could sense an impending explosion and I feared what Martin might do, so I said, "We could use a hand over here," but before I could finish the sentence, Martin had thrown the wrench to the pavement and was on the driver, asking, "What's the idea here?"

"Nothing." The driver shrugged, unintimidated. "Just chatting."

"That's my wife you're chatting to," Martin said.

"Yeah, she told me," the driver said, defiant. "So?"

The driver stepped back from the car and Martin pushed him into the road.

"Martin," Carol said, emerging from the limousine. She appeared relieved in a way that made her look like she'd come back from a year's vacation on a tropical island where the only real concern she'd had was whether to eat coconuts or bananas for breakfast.

A sound like a clap of thunder echoed and the driver was on the ground, writhing in the middle of the two-lane highway. A look of complete concentration overtook Martin as he kicked the driver in the chest. Carol froze where she stood and then a curious thing happened. Martin's face changed to real anguish, a deep hurt flashed in his eyes, a look in sharp contrast to the look on Dale's face when he had Shane right where he wanted him in the parking lot of the County Line. Dale's look was that of a champion, someone who was enjoying another's defeat at his hands. Martin, though, seemed truly pained as he continued to hammer his foot into the driver, who was by now curled up like a caterpillar on the road.

One of the Bandeses' neighbors happened by, picking us up, and the remainder of the trip was made in silence. I came to believe that Carol and Martin despised me in some way that I could understand and agree with. I parted company with them after we landed in Phoenix, excusing myself on some errand for the company but promising to see them at the Phoenician later that night.

But the look on Martin's face haunted me. When the hurt came across his face, you knew that everything his life was about was wrapped up in his life with Carol. He was protecting the source of his happiness, and you had the immediate feeling, watching him, that he understood that that happiness couldn't be found anywhere else and any threat or challenge to it would be met and extinguished.

Westfield Memorial Library
Westfield, New Jersey

As I watched Martin and his warrior-like battle with the driver, I was transported into the dreams of my youth, dreams where I used to see myself way into the future, married to someone who loved me. I dreamed those dreams as a way of comforting myself, I suppose. Talie had told me she'd had the same dreams. We both dreamed of a house, and a car, and a neighborhood where children would play under the afternoon shadows of elm trees. We could easily see ourselves in the windows of these homes on these tree-lined streets, in these phantom neighborhoods. Talie's dreams included enough children to people an entire elementary school, and my dream included similar scenarios. I'd imagine myself coming home from a good job, walking up the driveway, anticipating the warmth just inside the front door, where small coats hung on hooks and lunch pails with half-eaten sandwiches had been dropped next to unlaced shoes. Before anyone knew I was home, I could sense my family, anticipate their excitement when they saw me, an excitement matched in pitch only by my own. And inside our home, everything else in the world remained locked out, strange and foreign in the light of family.

The dream comes back to me with a clarity that is startling, mined from the darkness where dreams stir. Even if the details are the fantasies of youth, buried and forgotten in time, the truth of the dream remains. Dusted off, it gleams anew, and I'm embarrassed at how much I want to believe in it now, how much I want to believe it is something still worth trying for.

Westfield Memorial Library
Westfield, New Jersey

ACKNOWLEDGMENTS

....

My thanks to

Josephine Bergin

Rebecca Boyd

Stephanie Duncan

Heather E. Fisher

Tim Parrish

Michael Rosovsky

David Ryan

Elizabeth Searle

Lavinia Spalding

Dan Pope and everyone at Roundabout

Clarkes, Gilkeys, Kaliens, and Cottons

Mary Cotton and Max

Author photo by John Laprade

Jaime Clarke is a graduate of the University of Arizona and holds an MFA from Bennington College. He is the author of the novels *We're So Famous* and *Vernon Downs*; editor of the anthologies *Don't You Forget About Me: Contemporary Writers on the Films of John Hughes*, *Conversations with Jonathan Lethem*, and *Talk Show: On the Couch with Contemporary Writers*; and co-editor of the anthologies *No Near Exit: Writers Select Their Favorite Work from "Post Road" Magazine* (with Mary Cotton) and *Boston Noir 2: The Classics* (with Dennis Lehane and Mary Cotton). He is a founding editor of the literary magazine *Post Road*, now published at Boston College, and co-owner, with his wife, of Newtonville Books, an independent bookstore in Boston.

www.jaimeclarke.com

www.postroadmag.com

www.baumsbazaar.com

www.newtonvillebooks.com

Westfield Memorial Library
Westfield, New Jersey

ALSO BY JAIME CLARKE

VERNON DOWNS

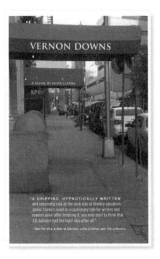

"*Vernon Downs* is a gripping, hypnotically written, and unnerving look at the dark side of literary adulation. Jaime Clarke's tautly suspenseful novel is a cautionary tale for writers and readers alike—after finishing it, you may start to think that J. D. Salinger had the right idea after all."

   – TOM PERROTTA, author of *Election, Little Children,* and *The Leftovers*

"Moving and edgy in just the right way. Love (or lack of) and Family (or lack of) is at the heart of this wonderfully obsessive novel."

   – GARY SHTEYNGART, author of *Super Sad True Love Story*

"All strong literature stems from obsession. *Vernon Downs* belongs to a tradition that includes Nicholson Baker's *U and I,* Geoff Dyer's *Out of Sheer Rage,* and—for that matter—*Pale Fire.* What makes Clarke's excellent novel stand out isn't just its rueful intelligence, or its playful semi-veiling of certain notorious literary figures, but its startling sadness. *Vernon Downs* is first rate."

   – MATTHEW SPECKTOR, author of *American Dream Machine*

Westfield Memorial Library
Westfield, New Jersey

"*Vernon Downs* is a brilliant meditation on obsession, art, and celebrity. Charlie Martens's mounting fixation with the titular Vernon is not only driven by the burn of heartbreak and the lure of fame, but also a lost young man's struggle to locate his place in the world. *Vernon Downs* is an intoxicating novel, and Clarke is a dazzling literary talent."

— LAURA VAN DEN BERG, author of *The Isle of Youth*

"An engrossing novel about longing and impersonation, which is to say, a story about the distance between persons, distances within ourselves. Clarke's prose is infused with music and intelligence and deep feeling."

— CHARLES YU, author of *Sorry Please Thank You*

"*Vernon Downs* is a fascinating and sly tribute to a certain fascinating and sly writer, but this novel also perfectly captures the lonely distortions of a true obsession."

— DANA SPIOTTA, author of *Stone Arabia*

Selected by *The Millions* as a Most Anticipated Read

"Though *Vernon Downs* appears to be about deception and celebrity, it's really about the alienation out of which these things grow. Clarke shows that obsession is, at root, about yearning: about the things we don't have but desperately want; about our longing to be anyone but ourselves."

— *The Boston Globe*

"A stunning and unsettling foray into a glamorous world of celebrity writers, artistic loneliness, and individual desperation."

— *The Harvard Crimson*

"*Vernon Downs* is a fast-moving and yet, at times, quite sad book about, in the broadest sense, longing."

— *The Brooklyn Rail*